THE SHUFFLING NIGHT

OFF SOUTH PRESS

ISBN 979-8-9851855-0-8

Also by Zachary Von Houser

Dreams of the Dead Night

THE SHUFFLING NIGHT

ISBN: 979-8-9851855-0-8

Front cover image by Zack Traum
Book design by Zack Traum

First printing edition 2021.

Off South Press

For Cacey
umqua

The Shuffling Night

It was like the unwritten rule with Starbursts. If someone offers you one, you grab the first one in line. You don't rifle through the pack for a specific flavor. Sometimes you get a strawberry, sometimes a lemon.

The first time I saw the house I wasn't blown away, but for ten thousand I wasn't really expecting something of memorable acclaim. From the little front yard grew a dogwood that had already lost its blos-

soms and seemed to be struggling against the weight of its remaining leaves. A flowerbed of unaligned stone ran from the side of the steps and housed a slimy bank of decomposing leaves and the dead stalks of long-forgotten lilies. White latex paint peeled from cedar siding and the window sills were the tunneled compounds of termite housing. A line of wilted ivy ran in a green vein upward through the center of the house. Still, standing back at the sidewalk and taking it in from the louvered window set in the extended gable to the rough stones of foundation, I could feel how perfectly it fit me. A great match need not be with something exceptional when you are content with how unexceptional your life has been.

It was a turning point, and probably the last one that I would ever have. Up to that time, it had been a life of odd jobs; bartender, laborer, kitchen worker, a little construction to fill out the nomadic resume. Just never anything stable or for

a long enough amount of time to become comfortable, to become established. No one ever tells you that stability might not stick, not ever. If I didn't own a bar or construction company by that point, if I hadn't figured out that tightrope to success, then I never would. It was the honest truth, and honesty and truth are exactly what they are, no matter if they fit into your expectations. There is no accounting for palatability in them. Now, I'm not sure how I would have felt about the house at any of the other points in my life, being so far removed from the person I was. But for this particular incarnation of myself, the fates had aligned. God damn them.

The basement was filled. All of those little things that accumulate over the course of one's life had ended up down there, then the next life after that. General debris, heartfelt mementos which, with the death of the mind endowing them with meaning, become worthless. I'm not sure how many people had come and gone in the life of the house, I'm only positive of one, but they all seemed to have left everything that they could at their departure. Bags of clothes spanning the generations; an old couch, missing most of its tan, plaid cushions; one of those clear, inflatable plastic chairs from the nineties, sitting as a pile of dry-rotted teal; a cotton clothesline hanging from the last bits of moldy thread; a pile of bug-eaten, leather yearbooks in one corner; a mound of old, yellowed paperbacks nearly to my shoulders in another. All of that greeted me in the first room after descending a low-ceilinged flight of treacherously smooth wooden stairs.

Through a little doorway of missing cinder block, was a larger, more dismal room. A wall of spiderweb clung to me as I traversed that entry for the first time. Where the first room had been lit by a convenient wall switch at the top of the stairs,

The Shuffling Night

I groped blindly in this room, my hands grazing mildewed joists, until I eventually found the little dangling piece of string activating a dull, yellow bulb. The only window that I could find, (though I would eventually find another buried behind an oak shelf) was of no use for light, as with the loss of one pane it had been quickly covered with a sheet of cardboard. Stopping nearby, I could feel the autumn breeze, in all of its rich decay, flowing in between strips of dried duct tape that flapped uselessly.

Tools, from fifty years ago or more, were piled or mounted with no apparent rhyme or reason throughout the room. A band-saw housing an extravagantly oblong spiderweb between its teeth, a drill-press so manual that I could discern no way that it had functioned. A row of hammers hung as only handles by loops of twine, with rusted heads laying as they had fallen on the floor.

On a tall, oak shelf covering more than

half of one wall, china had been packed as tightly as possible. Little cherubic faces, painted onto plates that leaned back, peeked over mounds of grime. Teacups were chipped or sat as piles of minuscule rubble. Pewter mugs dangled at the top, patinated and frothing with a brew of dust. The bare bulb swung a hangman's swing, giving everything an oscillating illumination that made the shadows dodge.

I retreated to the base of the steps, a dingy cheerleading uniform on a trash bag at my feet, and gazed over my sea of the forgotten. There was no way that I could afford to have it professionally cleared out, they'll gaze and plan every penny out of you, but it would only cost me time. Luckily, even though I was likely to be on my last drops of it, time was still free.

The whole house needed a round of renovations, to varying degrees of demand, but mainly needed work of a nature simple enough for even me to do. A new sub-floor and tile for the kitchen, refinishing

the floor in the dining room, hand-sanding and painting molding and trim all around. Although there was at least one fateful project that I was in no way skilled enough to do, I actually looked forward to the renovations at that time. Something, something of my own, that I could paint, and mold, and fashion into whatever form I desired. The first time in my life that I could say that, and with such freedom came an opening to the infinite that I had never known had been closed to me. It was like someone telling you to come inside as they stood along a plain brick wall, and suddenly, just as you were about to ask if they were mad, with a snap of fingers, a door appears. Like sin, or God, or love; the concept of any freedom is too abstract to see until you have, or have had, it.

I walked down cement steps that had never known a coat of paint or sealant, and into the back yard. To one side, an aggressively tall picket fence blocked the ground floor view of an equally aggressively tall

house for that neighborhood; to the other, a little split-rail fence of white suggested the property line without blocking the view of picturesque dogwoods and short apple trees, and a robin splashed in a mosaic-plated bath.

A path skirted around the side of the cement slab that filled half of the yard, and I obediently followed. Weeds worked across the path, full of thorns and the last mosquitoes of the year, their hyper wings flying into my ears and nose. I swatted and snorted, the barbed vines grown overhead scraping into my scalp, until I pushed through the low branches of a mulberry tree, its overripe berries bursting under my feet, and into a little concrete parking lot.

'Steve Sykes, CPA' was painted on the side of the little white building. The windows were dark, due to it being Saturday, or perhaps he was just an early closer. I never did find out which. The path continued along the side of the tiny parking lot,

to the back of the building. A large pond, or small man-made lake, sat there, unfinished and empty. Grass and weeds had reclaimed their land, now in long shallow banks. The spouts of water pumps spotted the lowest-lying ground, like black mushrooms. Mosquitoes buzzed around the depression, disillusioned at having their hopes dashed.

Returning to a survey of my land, the rutted, dirt driveway that ran along the side of the house ended at the concrete slab where, I can only imagine, once sat a shed. A wildly overgrown holly hid untold secrets beneath branches that swept down to the ground, its towering height casting a deep shadow to the fence. It was quickly decided that I had to remind it that we were in a civilized land, and it would be shaped accordingly. At the back edge of the property, blocking my view from the majority of the accountant's office, vines wove and interwove, between two spindly mulberries, their branches aflame with

dying leaves.

I carried a slice of pizza with me, a blob of orange translucence spreading across the paper towel beneath, and walked the guts of the house. 'Sight unseen' just means that you'll have to work your sight twice as hard once you get inside. I tapped and pressed at the wallpaper, waiting for the warning signs of crumbling plaster beneath. For as terrible as they were from outside, there weren't any signs of water damage beneath the window sills. Hair cracks ran through the ceiling, but anyone with plaster ceilings will tell you that that's a good thing to find, a can opener and a little spackle would have those sealed in no time; bad would have been chunks littering the floor and an open view of joists above. The toilet needed to be replaced, but I had, and still have, a thing about switching out toilets whenever I move into a place anyway. In the room next to the

bathroom, with ascending stairs at its far side, I found a bigger problem.

A cord was plugged into an outlet just inside the door, which was a little odd for a house unoccupied, but not impossible. It drooped to the floor, ran along the base molding, and seemed to disappear into the trim of the closet. I crouched down, noticing now that there was no hard edge to the outside of the trim, and dug my nail into the vanishing point. Layers of paint chipped away, a rainbow of decades-worth of hot colors; white, to beige, to black, to mauve, to burn orange, to royal blue, to grey. The nightmare that it must have been to cover some of those colors with others, but my own headaches were just starting. Finally, the cord was exposed as it worked its way upwards. I tugged lightly and a vein of cracks ran to the top of the trim. Slowly, I worked my way around the closet, along the base molding, and to the base of the stairs.

'Well... shit,' I thought, following the

path of the cord upwards.

At the top of the stairs, the cord ended, and three others extended outward from its outlet, spreading like scared roaches. The central cord ran straight back, giving the worn carpet runner a little wave, before turning into the empty back bedroom to the left. The cord on the right followed along the strange angles of the wall, hugging tight to where the pitched ceiling touched the floor, before cutting along the wall that framed the back room on the right. A little alcove sat at the top of the stairs, the banister as a barrier on one side, the wall to the room on the left as the other. In it was squeezed a little bed and table, without room for a hair to fall at either side. The ceiling pitched down to within a foot of the head of the bed, but how much room does your face need when you're sleeping? The third cord was stapled along the banister and vanished to somewhere between the short wall and bed frame.

Electricity was the one thing I wasn't

fool enough to do on my own. So, I went back down the stairs, pulled the cord from the outlet, and grabbed myself a beer. With the knob-and-tube wiring, and that splitting from one ancient extension cord to the rest, I was lucky I wasn't already running through a towering inferno, blotting out the flames in my thinning hair.

All things considered, within the varied history of home buying stories, especially sight-unseen, my finds hadn't been all that disconcerting. The walls still stood, inside and out; when I turned a knob, the water came out clean and only sightly off of clear; and, most importantly, the foundation and joists below the first floor were as sound as any could be found.

I went down into the basement, stepping over the cheerleading outfit, nearly toppling the precarious pile of yearbooks, and pulled a rusty lopper from its cocoon of cobwebs, their coat so thick that I could hear it tearing in the funerary quiet.

The cobwebs blew like witch's hair in the growing wind as I walked down the back steps, and the last rays of sunlight were being swallowed by a heavy, black bank of clouds coming in from the east. The temperature had dropped by nearly ten degrees since I had last been outside, and not a chirp or whistle could be heard from the birds. It was going to be a rough one.

I set to work quickly, not wanting to be caught in, if the chilled wind was any indicator, a cold rain. The branches of the holly were stubborn and heavy, their fibers letting out a groan as I pushed one aside to get the blades around another. I worked my way around the trunk, not too con-cerned about the health of the tree as I had never liked hollies all that much anyway, the sap dripping watery onto grass and the pile of branches growing.

It wasn't the prickling leaves or the blowing wind, but as I dragged a particu-

The Shuffling Night

larly fruitful branch toward the pile, something drew the hairs up on the back of my neck. I looked from one building to another for the eyes of a nosy neighbor peeking out of a darkened window, but could find nothing. It was my yard and I would do as I damned well pleased. Still, even these admonishments wouldn't relax my nervous skin. 'Maybe it was the pressure change,' I told myself.

It was then that a dark spot, in the corner of the yard, caught my eye. As I came closer, more spots came into view; a series of them clustered within the shade of the vines. They were the width of my thigh, deep holes extending out of blind darkness. I had never seen a gopher, or a groundhog, or any subterranean rodent of the area before, so I had no idea what the dimensions of their burrows would be. As I pondered that question, the first drop of rain struck my arm.

Along the shallow river of a road, cars rushed in the early evening grey, their

tires splashing waves across the side-walk. Where could so many people be in a rush to through suburbia? 'Don't bring a television or computer, they'll just be distractions,' I had thought before Tommy had picked me up and brought me down, you'll have plenty to do. Now, here I was, watching cars drive by for fun. I felt like some elderly shut-in, the eventual subject of neighborhood kids' dares, derision, and legends.

The holly looked like it was lifting its dress at me, the branches on the back still sweeping along the grass and giving it a dark, cavernous void. Once the weather cleared I would get back to evening it up. I drank a glass of water, more from boredom than anything, and looked into the refrig-erator. Twenty-three beers, some lunch meat, and bread. If all else failed, I could at least get blotto. I don't know, maybe I had become too accustomed to constant enter-tainment.

That night, I fell asleep on the couch,

the last thick ounce of beer in my hand and my phone playing Willie Nelson on the floor.

Grime and dirt caked under my nails, my arms a patchwork of browns and grey. I hauled an armload of books, their pages dropping like cherry blossom petals, from one corner to a series of short stacks in another. Trash, donate, keep, not sure, their heights sloping like bad stocks. Books with books, clothes with clothes, miscellaneous with miscellaneous. It was a tedious task, and with little reward, because whenever I would look over the room it wasn't as though anything had been cleared away. I couldn't see a spot of cleared floor and think to myself, 'see, we're getting there.' It was just a mess of a different shape. I would have liked to have donated all of the clothes, but after so many years of disregard and disuse in the basement, there wasn't a single piece unadorned by spots

of black mold or patches of mildew. I tried pushing from my mind what I must have been inhaling, but with that proving to be an impossibility, I did the only thing that I thought wise.

The rain ran down in a vicious little fall beside my foot, as I stood beneath the crooked awning, taking that first drag of my cigarette. I know, I know, I had quit for three years, and you don't have to give me that statistics. Why is it that everyone thinks that they are the only keepers of statistics, or facts like 'smoking isn't good for you'? I've never been tricked by tobacco companies, or big government, or aliens, into thinking that thick smoke pumping into my lungs was a good thing. I'm digressing pretty badly. It had rained all through the night and into that day. Puddles rippled with growth and the long leaves in the flowerbed next door drooped with the constant barrage.

It's odd how basements are lit on an overcast day. The rest of the house, the rest

of the world, on days like that seem to be locked into some surreal approximation of vision. The shadows aren't quite crisp enough, if they're there at all, the colors washed a little bit away. But a basement seems somehow sharper, as though the subterranean was glad to have any light at all, or that it was just basking in its view of the upper world knocked down a peg.

'Tomorrow, I'll take off those remaining branches,' I thought to myself. Peering around the corner, the spot where I had grabbed the lopper before was still a vacant slat in the dark. "Must have left it upstairs."

I went over to the book pile, picked out two that seemed promising, and headed upstairs. The clock on the wall said that it was just after four, though the window gave no hint other than that the sun still shone somewhere. A bit early to crack a beer, especially with the scratchy tail of a hangover still flicking in my mind; a bit too anxious to sit back and read just yet. I

pulled out an old, faded umbrella that I had found in the basement, opened the front door, and looked out to a place that I knew no more than forty feet of in any direction.

If not the most authentic, I thought that a good way to get a compact glimpse of the style of a town would be the main drag, the unimaginatively named New Jersey Avenue. Only a place with some semblance of the shared ideas of the place would have passed zoning, or at least the shared ideas of the elderly or bored enough to go to a zoning meeting. Either way, it would be quicker than a door-to-door census.

At first, there was just a string of your usual doctor's, dentist's and accountant's offices; all repurposed houses that, due to being on what became the main drag, weren't worth much as a home but could be sold at prime with the addition of a post to hang a sign. The funeral home was the only one of the group that held any interest to me, and that was due solely to its resemblance to the Amityville Horror house, and

maybe a slight curiosity toward the death industry in general. But who doesn't have that?

There was an old block wall, covered in decades worth of unkempt ivy running wild. Ivy's ivy, though, and variegation wasn't really my idea of a blast. At the end of the wall, it got a bit more interesting.

It's strange how things can suddenly loom. You would think that at a certain size it would be impossible for something to be inconspicuous, but then the world pulls a David Copperfield on you. The peek of the grey roof just showed across the top of the wall as I neared its end, and from there it seemed to grow from the ground at my approach. Windows slid upward from the tangle of unstoppable vines, then the very edge of a series of lower roof peaks.

I suppose it was because it was set so far back, deeper than I initially thought that the block went; that was how it could sneak up on me. It sat on the corner across a thin side-street, behind a cluster of sickly

shrubs and ratty grass, past a prematurely cracked parking lot housing a few cars that looked as though they hadn't moved in months or years. It was a Rationalist's dream, something that behind its thin layer of cheap siding and slate shutters must have once been an old penitentiary or a school for the mentally deranged. I could imagine where the swings would have sat; minds within a nightmare world trapped behind blank faces as their bodies made little arcs. It screamed of the place where you were sent because God or man had made you into something that couldn't be allowed to commingle with the rest of society. Just its sight told of weight, just a gluttonous block of impenetrability without permittance; wider and deeper than it was tall, and it was far from short. Five sets of little windows high at the center, four at the wings that flanked both sides. A little sign at the corner, framed by two shriveled begonias, said The Gardens; as though, through the commands of some

unexceptional advertisement, the struggling vegetation would be the dominant sight.

Breaking away from the behemoth, I found a dimly lit store of miscellany and craft supplies, a nail salon, locksmith, and at the end of the street, tucked into a patch of trees, a little garden center. The front of the store was set up like any florist's had ever been set up in the history of florist's, including the bundles of artificial flowers that had always seemed counter-intuitive to me. I slipped past the woman with purple-grey hair hunched over a handful of baby's breath with little more than a nod and through the door marked 'greenhouse' in bubble letters of carved wood.

The humidity and fragrance hit me like an ax, the weight of the perfumed air weighing down my lungs. I passed the orchids, which history showed to be impossible for me to keep alive; past the wide fronds of palms that would make me feel like I was living in some old Tarzan movie;

and into a far corner, not nearly as bright-
ly lit and, if the coating of tacky dust was
any indication, not nearly as often visited.
Beside a line of ficus clinging to their last
browned leaves, sat a juniper. Including the
pot, it was no taller than the length of my
forearm and, while long ignored and with
a crooked trunk, seemed to call my nostal-
gia. Something in its hopelessness, among
these wondrous flowers, and colors, and
exotic smells, reawakened the lonely child
of my past.

The rain had ceased as I stepped onto
the parking lot, and in the new quiet, the
sounds of deeper waters could be heard. I
walked a quiet path toward the sound, the
potting soil unwieldy like a bag of buck-
shot under my arm, and the potted juniper
sitting within another pot tight against
my chest with the other. The rock and
sand path crunched underfoot as I passed
a forgotten shed to the side of the center.

Wild bushes that had once been weeds grew amorphous at either side and swirling gulls called overhead. I could smell it growing stronger in the air, renouncing the exhaust of the highway and artificiality of industry in those last few feet, as the unseen spray began to fleck my face.

It extended there, grey-green and rushing, the waters of the back bay, pressing and forcing channels through the bay grass, foaming and gurgling where it hit the thin stalks and slimy mud. I craned precariously over the edge of the seawall, testing my footing with each passing degree, the wide expanse of openness demanding always a little more. Something new, something beautiful to explore.

I went through the line of plates meticulously. A little shepherd boy with a lamb; a pair of children with oversized heads, kissing beside a tree stump, as though that wasn't creepy to look at; a little hunter hugging a deer, vibrant hearts rising from their heads. They all came upstairs with me. I placed them into a plastic bag in the sink and tied the handles tight. It wasn't completely unsatisfying to feel the meat tenderizer come down, imagining their little faces cringe and scream as the realization of collision became clear. The porcelain shattered high-pitched and fast, slivers jotting through the plastic in revolt of their confines. I gave it five or six taps, the mound in the bag transforming before my eyes, until I supposed the job was done.

I poured the fragments over a circle of screening that I had found in the basement and placed at the bottom of the pot. A few quick shakes and I assumed all of the dust and tinier shards had fallen out. I poured the little granules from the innards of a bunch of water filters into a bowl of the potting soil and gravel, assuming it had to have some carbon in it. In went the mix, which I left uncompacted besides an inch or so at the bottom. It would have been

better if I had sphagnum moss and coco fiber instead of potting soil, but you can only ask so much of a place like that.

Most of this would have been unnecessary if I had bothered to check the bottom of the pot for a hole at the shop, or if I felt like bothering to drill a new one, but neither of those were in the cards at that time. As it was, if I didn't want the roots to rot, it would need someplace for the extra water to escape to. There aren't too many things that I can claim to know like the back of my hand, but after years of trying to have a halfway decent looking place, only for it to turn into a forgotten produce stand, I'd figured out how to keep a plant from drowning at least.

I shook the soil free, trimmed down the longer stretching roots, and placed the plant into its new home. A quick run of water to get the growth going, and I placed it on the lonely table by the window in the living room. Any companion deserves a name, and this was no different. Oscar,

that was a good name for the formerly forgotten. It didn't hurt that he was also scroungy green and everyone seemed to think he was trash.

The cheeseburger that I'd had delivered washed down relatively easily with the help of a Red Stripe. The fries were an over-salted pile of sogginess sitting beside the translucent sheets of lettuce I had pulled from the cheese. I wondered how many times the lettuce had been frozen and thawed for it to have gotten to that state. It's strange, the things your mind wonders when you're alone.

Little dimples scattered across the carpet, left behind by a previous owner, by furniture that must have sat there for decades. You could picture how it must have looked by the distance between recesses, a chair here, a love seat there, cozy and packed just tightly enough. Now it was just a painting of vacancy, an ornately patterned lunar landscape. Just me, the carpet, Oscar's little table, and a couch

that I had dragged to and from my last five apartments to fill the room.

Glancing at the table, I noticed a little spot of brown mixed into Oscar's needles. I didn't buy him to win any awards, but my general knowledge of horticulture told me that they couldn't be helping with his general well being.

The light from the accountant's office flickered an ambient Morse code through the lace kitchen curtains and the radiators let off a series of pops to announce their emergence from hibernation, as I dug through a pile of pocket tools on the counter.

I slowly pushed the razor through the base of the little branch, and to the callus of my thumb, pulled away the desiccated limb and placed it onto the table. The little missing pocket looked a bit odd, but that would grow back out.

He didn't look like any professional bonsai, there was no intrinsic artistic value or premeditated flow to the branches, but

that was the closest thing that I could think of. At least he didn't appear to be nestled to Death's bosom.

As one track on a Hank Williams play-list ended, (it was mostly Senior, some-times the Third, never Junior) I thought that I heard a sound, like some distant dog scratching to get in. I pulled my phone from the empty pint glass, hit pause, and listened, but only the light pops of the radi-ators in the hollow rooms spoke.

I lay in bed, unused to the quiet. Every-where that I had ever been before had had something; the studio above the Mexican restaurant, where the music would blare after they had 'officially' closed for the night and their business actually began; the two-bedroom workingman's apart-ment with paper-thin walls that afforded overly-loud sex into one bedroom, or the drunk that switched between wailing or raging against the world from the other;

the trinity on a 'cozy little street' as the property manager had said, where kids would have fun smashing beer bottles or firing off shots long into the night. In that little bed, framed in tightly, there was nothing but the soft hum of cars occasionally passing the opposite side of the house, quiet enough to be considered natural ambiance.

Patterns of shadows from the mulberry leaves outside worked kaleidoscopic on the pitched ceiling just above my head. They would drop into a sheet of darkness and then reemerge, seemingly more clearly defined, as the motion detector at Skykes' perceived a new potential threat. I watched the swirling dark, my mind losing focus as it found patterns and stories in their shapes. Eyes became mountain peaks became sleeping cats became eyes. Slowly, the patterns became less pattern, the stories more dominant, my eyes settled shut for longer periods, when something caught my ear. I was so deeply transfixed

by half-sleep that, although I recognized that there was a noise, my mind refused to acknowledge it.

'Just a little longer,' I thought, and in response to my silent pleas the noise came again. A little clearer, now that I was that much more awake. A rustle, soft but distinct. I went up on my elbow, the old springs creaking under my weight. Beyond my feet, the little desk and chair waited silently in the darkness that embraced them at most times under the corresponding slant. The light died, and in the darkness I waited. My lungs sounded clumsy and loud without eyes to distract me. There it was again, in that gap between breaths, a slow, steady rustle from one of the open entries to the other rooms on that floor. A long silence, and then the rustle, and then another long silence.

I added pruning tree branches that touched the roof to my list of things to do, and turned my back to the tenebrous rooms, tucked my forearm under the

pillow, and watched the shadows play on the curtain until sleep decided to return.

I dreamed of a misty void. It was me and her, I wasn't sure of who this 'her' was, but I knew that I had to tell her. She was somewhere in her early twenties, or a month or two shy of, her hair a messy bob, just the top of her jacket floating above the mist. The youth emanated, an indefatigable energy streaming out. It wasn't bright or dark where we were but a colorless nothing, with the mist even taking away the definitiveness of eternity. I would start to speak, but each time, before I could utter a sound, she would say 'shh,' slow and reserved. The mist played off of the waves of her blonde hair, snaking through and drifting its flaxen lightness. I knew I had to tell her. I knew that it was my one goal, but each time her silencing 'shh' was unarguable. Over and over, just that one noise without dispute. It paralyzed my voice box, and as I stared into her dull-blue eyes a resignation dropped over me.

A restless sleep isn't always better than no sleep at all. I woke to a chill coursing over me, my flesh running in waves of goosebumps. I rubbed my right eye and glanced down to the blankets in a crumpled ball at my feet. It felt like I could almost see my breath, and when I breathed in deep to attempt it, there was something lingering in the air. It was bitter, and almost familiar, though too vague to pinpoint.

I needed something for breakfast, something I knew well, something that would comfort to shake the strange grogginess from my mind. With that grogginess, there was the hint of a bitter depression far off in the distance, but close enough to feel its effects. I didn't want to explore, or venture, or much of anything, and if there had been anything resembling the ingredients of a breakfast at home I would have happily stayed in. As it was, there wasn't, so I was forced to venture forth.

The Shuffling Night

The first fallen leaves rustled by at my feet and, though it was still relatively warm, I could smell some wood fire off in the distance. Maybe it was a burning pile of leaves. I'm not sure if that was still legal there. I glanced up at the house, its strips of peeling paint and all, at the walkway lined with bricks laid on their corners like the ridges of a crocodile's back, and headed down the street.

I turned onto the street that ran parallel to the main drag, but a block before it. Perhaps an anonymous block, just like every other suburban block would hold with it, although unknown, the feel of a place understood. I could see the gargantuan Gardens, and the backs of the offices, but between the two, instead of the rough rock wall, there was a new chain link fence.

Shade and quiet dominated. I walked along an overgrown flagstone path, pine trees casting dagger shadows across my way. It was a cool, windless place and felt as though no matter what season it would

always be that temperature, that still. From this side, the stone wall was even more covered with ivy, its materials all but impossible to tell. It smelled the way I imagined an abandoned castle would smell, fresh and clean but older than a single life could be. Acorns were scattered across the path, squirrels scurried from branch to branch, and headstones were laid in imperfect rows along the undulating grounds. A little opening sat in the wall at the far end, which I hadn't noticed the day before, and I was back in the world.

The creamed chipped beef with a side of fries was hanging about as heavily in my hand as they would soon be in my stomach as I reached the corner. The house stood there, warm and comforting, and any second-guessing of getting take-out was immediately banished. I rubbed my eye, thinking that there must have been grit or an eyelash in it and, as I pulled my

hand away, I saw the living room curtain swaying back into place.

After searching for a possible cause for the draft, and finding more of them than I wanted, I stood at the counter with my breakfast quickly congealing into a brick of white and pink. The neighbor stood in his yard, the bald top of his head a newborn pink, spotted with the brown splotches of approaching death. Shoulders sagged forward and, as he bent toward his birdbath, a line of ridges like a mountain range ran down the back of his white shirt. He scooped into the bath, his hand covered by a dirty teal glove, pulling handfuls of dripping brown leaves. I could see him examining the holly, with its dumb train of branches on the one side, his neck craning and giving him a more decrepit appearance. As he straightened up and head turned toward my window, I gave a little, slow wave, but he just kept turning and started for his house.

"Why's there always some old asshole

in the suburbs?" I said.

I continued on with the steady rhythm of clean, bag, move, in the basement throughout the day. It was a deep sea of haze that filled the air, the light bulb like a halo in the murk. It didn't seem like there would ever be any progress, but with the mountain of trash bags, there were slowly forming islands of floor between. At the end of the day, my skin felt like it squirmed in its enrobed grime but, though it was far off, nothing was stopping or slowing the progress toward completion.

It was night by the time I ascended the stairs. I hadn't noticed the churning of time somehow and, though I thought I had only been a couple of hours, when I checked my phone it said that it was after eight. The little red glyph in the corner also told me that my battery was nearing depleted.

"Shit, where'd the time go?" I asked.

The rain was still holding off for the time being but the clouds, fat, heavy clouds that blocked out sky and star, threatened

to tear apart and flood us at any time. To think of how innocuous things seem at the time. I walked into the darkened dining room and felt along the wall for the switch.

With my phone plugged in next to the couch, I attempted to read, but between the dry warmth and the comfort of the cushions I had trouble keeping my eyes open. There are fights worth fighting, and those that winning will give no gains. At my age it was easy to realize that there was little reason to fight a good sleep, so without a second thought I put the book down, poured out the rest of my beer, and promptly headed up the stairs.

I woke in a fog, the darkness a shroud that seemed to have a texture as it bathed me. I didn't know what had awakened me, but it had come like a shot. I lay there, some lizard-brain part alert. My sinuses

stung and there was a tingle in the corner of my right eye. Then it came, that which must have awakened me.

A sound came from the other side of the attic, that hushed rustle from the night before. It was like the soft drone of static, back when static still existed; as though someone in another room had forgotten to turn off a television in a drunken haze. How many, of whatever verminous creature it was, would it take to make such a constant noise? I listened to it, entranced in the overlapping rapid scratches, until the shift.

It came suddenly. First, the scratching slowed, the scrapes tinkling away. The silence was an eternal second, the longest moment between heartbeats. I lay, stopped mid-breath. Then came the screech. It pierced my eardrums. It flooded the room. I pushed back, out of instinct, the small of my back digging against the banister. The thud, I felt it through the bed, into my bones.

The Shuffling Night

I reached hesitantly across the bed. My fingers brushed the edge of the table. I stretched farther, felt the ancient doily, its pattern a guide for my search. Silence. I could feel the moisture between my fingers. It was only as my fingertips touched the far edge that I realized the futility of my search. My phone still lay on the floor downstairs, plugged into the wall.

I dropped my feet tenuously onto the floor. My breathing was a jagged grate. As I eased off of the bed, the squeal of its springs caught my breath in my throat. I'm not sure what I expected to find. Every groan of floorboards was a tidal wave of sound. I let my hand run along the wall to keep me in line. My eyes ached with their struggle for light. The two rooms were the great muzzles of long-dead beasts.

"I'm a grown man," I said in a whisper that came out as tumbling shale.

How do you decide which door? I had never fully grasped the weight of the trope in movies or stories. Door number one

or two? Which one holds the lion, which sanctuary? My right fist clenched on its own, and that was enough to make the decision for me. I turned into the room, hand raised, unsure of what I would find, so unprepared for anything at all.

A stillness that only utter emptiness can emit surrounded me. My body told me, as much as my straining eyes, that nothing lurked in the dark. Nothing was perched or crouched to spring upon me, because there was nothing from which to spring. Just a hollow set of walls that made me feel like a fool.

I walked to the door of the other room more casually, the tension shattered, and scanned an equal emptiness.

Glancing into the windows across from me, the old man sat there, fingers feebly tapping at the computer. It was one of those older models, with the big, boxy monitor and everything in that sad shade of beige.

I'm not sure what the latest models would have even looked like but I knew that that wasn't it.

What could he have been doing? I wasn't some young buck, so it amazed me even that much more that this old man, with his paunch hanging out of the bottom of a t-shirt every time that I saw him, and his frail strands of white hair that looked like they would melt in the rain, could have any interest in even very outdated technology. Why go breaking your back every day at a factory, a fishing boat, or surveying some uncharted plots of land under the brutal sun, just to end up as some sad, old fuck looking up a plot point to an episode of Murder She Wrote from decades before?

A loud crash pulled me from my thoughts, and I rushed from the kitchen. In the back room, shards of reflection scattered across the floor, bouncing back the dingy drab of the ceiling. At the base of the stairs sat the frame of the mirror that had hung next to the window just

above. 'Eh, that was an accident waiting to happen anyway,' I thought and went for the dustpan and brush.

I'd grown more conscious of the time when I was in the basement. A corner of my sight stayed on the window, keeping track of the passage of hours. Old memories would sneak in, trying to steal the whole of my thoughts, to trap me within their world of the inconsequential past, and *that* I had to stay vigilant over because one path would lead to another and darkness would come before I had noticed.

The shadow of the house told me that it was around five o'clock, the peak of the roof nearing halfway up the neighbor's fence. I stepped over the cheerleading outfit and went upstairs for my lunch. Lunch had been getting pushed back farther and farther over the last couple of days, in relative accordance with how much later I had been waking. I chalked it up to having no set time that I had to get up for work, and assumed that was just a

more natural time for my body to wake. All the better.

I drank a glass of water and for an instant couldn't figure out how old Molly must have been at that point, when a pinprick of pain jolted in my eye. It was just an instant, but with that new focus, I noticed how sensitive it actually felt, the grit that seemed to be flowing below the lid.

The light over the bathroom sink flickered a worrying flicker as I brought my face close to the mirror. It wasn't anything obvious, nothing that I would have picked up from across the room, nor anything that would have stuck out if it was someone else's eye and I was having a long conversation with them. But it was my own, and I knew how it was supposed to look. On the bottom lid of my right eye, in toward the duct, was a spot of slightly darker pink. I pulled the lid away, tearing up at the little jab of pain as the suction broke, and looked around. No eyelashes or scratches to the eye were clearly visible. So, with no known culprit, I decided it must be something in the dust and grime hovering in the basement air. I rinsed as well as I could and hoped that there was some elixir in the water to make the discomfort worth it.

I pulled a slice of pizza from the refrigerator and poured another glass of water. The grease had congealed a deep amber atop the cheese, the crust curled upward and a grey-tan. It looked sad, but lunch pizza always looks sadder than dinner pizza, even when it's fresh. There must be something to the magic of pizza night in childhood that reflects back through your whole life. Maybe that's why it's never quite as appealing to eat before nightfall, and why the person making it never seems to put the same care into your two o'clock order as they would your six.

Either way, I had neither the advantage of freshness or timing, but that wasn't what bothered me. That feeling

had returned. No matter the direction I faced, I felt that vague premonition of the hunted. Some eyes, somewhere, peering at me with an intensity that was tangible. Through the windows, I inspected every gap between branches, every shadowy corner, every curtained window for a sign of life, but could find nothing. Trying to cast away the feeling as a fool's fancy did nothing to dispel it. Some deep instinct of survival hinted that I was being observed. I pulled the curtains against the world and ate quickly, hunched over the sink.

Perhaps the loneliness was getting to me. Perhaps it was remorse. Perhaps I was feeling that human need for social contact, no matter the context. After all, for all of the remoteness that I felt, I may as well have been on Nova Zembla.

I worked my way through a series of twisting, darkened streets. Canadian geese called down from their silhouetted

formation against the grey sky. The wind was a continuous bully pushing me along as I tracked the directions on my phone. The distraction, the vapidness, the pointless validation; for all of the things that annoyed me about the world's fixation over these little, greedy rectangles, they did have a few helpful features.

At a rise in the street, traffic swarmed by with a consistency of yellow headlights that made the world seem that much more drab. When the light finally changed, I crossed over, made a little bend in the street, and down below sat stretched out an inkblot-test of the bay wilds. A pair of fishing boats were tugging into port between a line of wavering channel markers, their horns bounding in, muted with the absorbed moisture. I cracked open a beer in preemptive victory and headed down the steeply sloping road.

My boots dried in the vestibule, their

lower halves coated in a slimy, dead-brown mud that emanated sulfur and salt and the amalgam of all things that ever happen in that murky wash, and the socks which had also soaked sat in a pile at their side. Tiny needles fell into Oscar's pot as I trimmed out a new spot of brown and attempted to work the shape into something that might be mistaken for planned cohesion. The nail scissors that I had bought from a corner store seemed to do an alright job of things, but my stout and battered fingers had trouble maneuvering with such delicate precision.

"Alright, maybe just a little from the right," I said, as a smell wafted into the room and I jumped up from the milk crate on which I was seated.

A thin, slithering trail of smoke was gliding from the kitchen doorway, caressing the dining room ceiling as it spread. I ran through the living room and into the dining room, feet dragging slightly to stop myself from slipping on the smooth floor,

cursing quietly to myself.

My mind must have been somewhere else, divided between the burning last slice of pizza in the oven; the seemingly endless fight to ward off Oscar's demise; some noise that I half-heard from upstairs; and the return of a rain that seemed to swirl perpetually above the area, leaving for only brief sojourns of relaxation to amplify its strength. Either way, my focus was somewhere else during my third or fourth dragging step that I took into the dining room.

I felt the point enter, but not directly; in that inconsequential way that your body registers something happening when there is already too much going on to begin with. Like a fly hovering in the corner of the movie screen as a bomb goes off. That delayed registering was just a little too slow to stop my pendulous feet, and by the time they did, it was too late. I could audibly hear the snap of the wood, I could feel the spring of flesh released from

tension. My foot rolled of its own accord and I took a few staggering steps before I could stop myself, hand braced against the wall.

I hobbled over to a chair that sat against the wall. It barely protruded from the sole of my foot, as wide as a quarter and tapering at the top. I dug my nail down for as much grip as I could manage on the splinter, my toes curling from the fire that flowed from it.

The popping, that vile popping, of the ridges of wood as it slowly emerged from my tissue. I could feel every groove as I pulled. With every fraction of success, I couldn't believe that there could be any more to come. At least I could see it thinning in its dagger's blade. A bead of sweat dropped from my brow, I found a more solid grip, and forced a quick jerk through my muscles.

A thin dribble of blood ran from the opening, hitting the dusty floor and splashing little flecks of burgundy onto my other

foot. The wound was an oven, heating every millimeter of the wound's depth. I looked down at my hand, the hole in my foot dripping a slow drip of blood onto my calf, and saw the inch and a half of jagged wood that had been so firmly embedded in me. After the distressing problem with my eye, I had been looking for a new project to give me time to recuperate from the dust, and now I was quite sure that I had found it. I pulled at my foot to get a better look at the wound, and the burn intensified with the blood bubbling up like crude oil and spilling over the arch of my foot.

"Fuck!" I shouted, and heard that shuffle and thud from above in response.

The rain. That monotonous, windless rain, under clouds devoid of variation, which seemed to confine like a coffin. Leaves ran through the water washing along the curb, flame-colored ships to the siren's song. I felt the vibration of rain-

drops through the handle of my umbrella as I walked along New Jersey Avenue. The little ornate lampposts were lit, though it wasn't even noon.

The hardware store was as you'd find any small-town hardware store, a bit too cramped, a bit too overstocked for the amount of space available. Just walls of gadgets, slightly overlapping each other with fading price tags haphazardly adhered across their packaging, and textured cement floors, like you were already back in your garage. Some kid, wearing an oversized, red smock and obviously forced into labor by his proprietor parents, trailed ten feet behind me the whole time. Apparently, the over-fifty crowd was known for their waves of flagrant theft in town.

I settled on a hand sander that looked like it had been stocked on the shelf while Chernobyl was still humming away, a stack of sandpaper, and some polyurethane that

still sounded fluid when I shook the can. I dodged the kid for a little while, turning the corner at the end of one aisle only to turn back before I hit the next, turning around and walking toward him to see if he would backpedal. It's not that I assumed he was a twelve-year-old asshole, which he very well may have been, but I wanted him to have something slightly interesting happen in the dullest pits of hell to which he was condemned. Dick Tracy finally laid off and wandered away when I reached his father at the counter, a man a little younger than me with a face fit for Reagan's campaign posters.

I stopped in the parking lot, a few feet from two guys standing by an old, weathered pickup truck, and contemplated until I came to the conclusion that a soggy time with a cigarette was better than a dry one with cravings. I sat my umbrella down, transferred the paper bags to one arm, and pulled out my pack.

"So, I told her he can't just be disre-

specting me like that. I ain't gonna put up with it. Especially not in my own house," the older of the two said.

"Shit. But what are you gonna do? Sam's her brother, and if she didn't cut him off for that other shit, what makes you think something like this will?"

What the hell did Sam do?

"I'm not talking about her cutting him off. She'll go to work and I'll just pull his lazy ass aside then."

"I don't know... I'm not sure I'd want to be pulling him aside anywhere that there ain't a bunch of witnesses." The younger one fidgeted with his keys.

"Hot damn! He goes away for a little bit and everyone's scared shitless of him. Under that muscle and his shitty old tattoos, he's still the kid that shit his pants because we wouldn't let him into the school after recess."

"If you say so. I'd sleep light for a week after that though."

It was then that I realized that I had

been listening for that whole time. Why was I listening? I didn't know these people. We had never met, and in all likelihood never would meet. But something in the melodic cadence of speech, just simple human dialog, gripped me magnetically.

I put out my cigarette, rubbed my eye, and cleared my throat, picking my umbrella up from the puddle in which it sat.

A cardinal stood on the windowsill as I wedged scraps of cloth from the basement under the legs of the battered china cabinet. It pulled its neck down deep between wings that smoothly transitioned from a brilliant crimson to a grey-garnet, flecks of rain in the wind catching in its plumage and running down its peaked beak. Across the fence, its bath was a waterfall of murk and detritus, splashing mud across its base. A wind rattled its way along the house and, with the first shiver of the windowpane, off the bird flew.

The Shuffling Night

Though, at the time, it seemed as though there could be nowhere in the world for it to find comfort for its brittle bones.

It had been just under twelve years since I had seen Molly. She'd probably already had a family of her own, perhaps a kid of her own on the way, and with the dagger memories of her old man quickly fading away with the growth of her new life. Those things happen, I knew then as I know now. It had happened with my old man as well and I didn't blame her.

I hadn't been the best when she had come around. Not that I was any different now, because I now know that people just don't change like that. There isn't always some great, shining moment that transforms your very essence into the person that television or a preacher says that you should be. Sometimes the person that you make your first cognitive thoughts as is the person that you're stuck as. Age or reminiscences be damned, the life that you're brought up into, and the life that you bring

others up into isn't always going to be a life with harps and a beautiful glow in the background.

I knew the cut of my cloth, and it was of fibers that wouldn't stretch into a form fit for a family. I knew that I would always be the type without a tether, would always go the speed and direction that my specific type of life demanded, and that anyone attempting to hold on and steer would be torn bit by bit. So, I did the only thing that seemed reasonable. I left.

It wasn't some 'I'll be right back. I'm going for a pack of smokes,' sort of thing. I had sat Erin down in our little apartment, Molly on the carpet a few feet away playing with a wooden train that was missing a wheel, and told her how things would be if I stayed. I laid down the detriments pretty thickly, because that's what you do when you're a self-interested prick like I am, and the very small group of positives. She was still youthful and could find someone new to keep her company. Molly

was so young that she wouldn't remember it as a full memory; it wasn't as though she were already a teenager and would develop some impenetrable complex from the whole thing and end up in a flophouse. They could start over. Begin again, but this time along a path that would lead to serenity, to some semblance of comfort and happiness that my eventual raging and resentment would never allow if I was locked in with them. I've always been pretty good at painting a picture, if it means that I'll get my way. A dog is a dog, even if you paint some spots, glue on horns, and tell him how great being a bull will be.

Two visits a year seemed as fair as I could expect and, to be honest, as much as I could handle. So, I bought an old pickup with a rebuilt engine dropped in that was a little too small, loaded my meager possessions into the back, and headed south. A thousand miles and festive cocktails as far as the eye could see seemed like enough for a fresh start, and I had always hated the

damned snow anyway.

Molly would come down, some pretty stewardess guiding her out along the way from the plane by her little hand, and we would head to whichever decrepit efficiency I was staying at, at the time. There two weeks would pass, with me working as little as whatever boss I had at the time would allow. A block or two to walk to the beach, half a pint of vodka in my iced tea bottle, we would while the days away. Out at the surf early, a light snack of whatever was on sale packed; out to some bay or seawall to catch a lunch of crabs with some old, smoked turkey necks for bait; a six-pack and some television with dinner. A couple of weeks of this at a time, then I would walk her back to her gate at the airport, she would take the hand of some pretty stewardess, and I would be back in my Peter Pan life with a few tears on my cheeks. The early days were easier.

Eventually, she got older, and I got a little worse at fighting for time off at

the bar or site that I was working at. The nagging thoughts about this would build and a bottle of something or other was the only way that I thought to wash away their foundations, until I would be passed out by nine most nights. Changes chipped away, year by year, with her staying out on her own more during visits and me drinking away regret until eventually, the chasm between us was too great to ignore or span. I didn't understand her. I didn't understand the world or the culture in which she had grown and currently lived. Her hair, her clothes, the things that she called music, it was all so far from what I had decided was objectively cool. I was too dumb or scared to try and figure it out.

The first time that Molly only came down once in a year was when she was fifteen. It was only two weeks before she was due to visit when Erin called me and told me that Molly was going to some friend's parent's campsite for the summer. A conversation building into a screaming

match ensued, me berating Erin, probably unfairly, for not living up to our agreement, her bringing up the fact that I was the one who had decided to leave in the first place, until she was cut short mid-sentence. Molly's voice, a shouting sob, broke in, telling me that she was the one who wanted to go and why wouldn't I let her live her life and that it's not like I cared or we even did anything anyway when she had to come down. 'Had to come down,' that's what it ended with. A cluster of words like a sledgehammer to my sternum.

That summer I met Jenny, that horrible trick of fate. Molly came down the next winter, and we tried to make things seem as though none of that had happened, but the line had been drawn and we could feel it even if we didn't look. She met Jenny and tried to pretend to like her, and Jenny tried to pretend that she liked Molly back, but neither was a good liar. Jenny stayed at a friend's house for most of the visit, claiming that it was so that there could be a little

'family time'.

The next spring, after an afternoon of heavier than usual drinking, Jenny slipped out of the house while I was passed out, came back in with me snoring in the same position, opened the top drawer of my dresser, and closed it without so much as a sound. I can't really blame her as much as I'd like to. She had been having ideas that some secret girlfriend of mine was hiding under the bed at night, or in the hamper as we ate breakfast, and more than once I had walked in to her stabbing between the weaves of the wicker hamper with a chef's knife. I still don't know if it was a build-up of years of drug use, or if she had been going just a little harder at the time, but that'll happen.

So, I was still passed out on the couch, my pants undone with the legs bunched high around my calves, when the door came in. It was screaming, and lights, and gun barrels in my eyes, and a horrible taste in my dry mouth. They threw me from the

couch and had my wrists zip-tied behind my back before I could think of a word to say. With my face pressed into the sandy carpet and a bottle cap under the couch staring me in the eye, I suppose I seemed less of a threat because the lights and guns were lowered, the shouts brought down to barking questions. Where was it? What? Did I think I was smart? Did I think they wouldn't get me? I didn't have the object of the questions, so I didn't have an answer.

A shout came from my bedroom. An officer came out with a sandwich-bag full of what turned out to be pain killers and ecstasy. I could see that Jenny's dresses and purses were gone from the closet behind him and knew that I was thoroughly fucked.

None of my prints were found on the bag, and the partials that were on there didn't match me, so they couldn't put me away for as long as they had hoped. At least my public defender was adept enough to get that right. But, without me rolling over

The Shuffling Night

on anyone, not even her, the judge still had a smile when he gave me my five years.

People think that prison is all fight scenes in the yard or dropping the soap, like some hyper-dramatized movie where they take a pretty actor and give him a few really fake looking tattoos and some stubble and think he looks like your generic con. Really though, it's just a bunch of guys trying to fight off boredom and the thoughts that can grow in exponents in your skull until you're ready to bash your head into the wall just to have some semblance of autonomy. Sure, there might be a few hard-line racists, just like your church bake-sale probably has a few hard line racists, but not every guy that steps out on parole has an iron eagle decapitating jews and blacks across his chest under the dumb t-shirt he was arrested in.

It the lack of an ability to relate on a situation in the outside world is what really

gets you. There's no common bond, and after so long having that to fall back on, it's hard to find a subtler form of experience. Back there it was easier, 'hey! You're in prison? Me too! What a coincidence'. No matter what you were, and what you hated before, when it comes down to a potentially volatile moment inside you always have the guards, the walls, the lawyers and judges to rally against together. It's amazing what the bond of mutual hate can do for you.

They main thing I want you to gather from this is that not every prison is San Quentin, Attica, or Folsom. For the most part, for a lot of us that spent our time in no-name prisons in no-name America, it's just the longest, most boring detention you've ever had at school.

I was trying to talk a black kid called Slips into giving me what barely passed for a cigarette, and explaining the glory that

was Bruce Springsteen's Nebraska, when the news came. Erin had been having some health problems for the last few years. She had never been the model of health, but recently touches of flu and every sort of malady had been befalling her. I figured that it was stress, or not giving herself enough rest or food, or any sort of thing that the bare minimum of contemplation would provide, but I was just sitting there when C.O. Murphy told me that she was dead.

I didn't have any bad thoughts toward Erin, and I assumed, and still vaguely do in some rose-colored version of myself, that she didn't either. I suppose even if I did have some ill will, she was still the mother of my child and that counteracts a good deal of animosity. Cancer, and especially pancreatic cancer, cares not about emotion though, and in that way, its motivation has some level of purity. A motivation that I had never felt the slightest inkling of. So, that news, and the knowledge that it had

been hidden from me, was a long, jagged blade into my gut.

The phone rang with only the machine to answer each time I was allowed to use the phone, that same mechanical message for me to blather at. Day after day, I waited in line, made my call, and walked away disheartened, praying that the next time Molly would pick up. I never knew what I would say, but I hoped that some paternal instinct would kick in and unlock the inspirational reassurance that she needed to hear.

Three months is a long time to talk to no one, and an even longer time to have no idea what you would say otherwise. Then one day, after I dialed the number something had changed, not in the 'Dad, thank you so much for calling' way that I had been hoping for, but with a different mechanical voice telling me that the number I had dialed had been disconnected. Erin's parents, which I assume Molly went with, seemed to have vanished. I tried to find

some way to get her number; any channel that I could think of just a flash of instantly dimming hope.

For the next three years, I drifted through, a visage of myself through fogged glass. I move from cell to cell, each one a bit more cramped than the last, without a hint of complaint. The food even more tasteless and grey than it had been before. Even on the day that they realized how overcrowded we were, and I got that stamp of freedom on my sheet, I stumbled out tired and old.

Someone once told me to look her up on social media, but I can't make heads or tails of it. No Molly with Erin's last name or mine could be found anywhere. What would I say anyway?

It was in that far-off place, the memories falling around me without order or reason, like an explosion in a leaf pile, that I twisted my foot in a certain way and felt any healing that had occurred tear with a spurt of blood.

I pulled the furniture across the room one piece at a time; my only illumination was a sun that would bend and blear and list behind the gauzy clouds of a New Jersey sky. From time to time a rhythmic tapping came from the ceiling, but I blocked it with work in the way that I had for those three years. I couldn't let my mind chip itself away. This was no time for delusion to set in. It was only when I caught myself chewing the nails of one hand as I pulled a chair out of the room with another, that I realized I could probably use a cigarette break.

The cardinal was nowhere to be found, but still, my eyes scanned over branch and fencepost for some little company. As a long tube of ash fell from my cigarette and into the puddle at my feet, the hairs on the back of my neck stirred. My perception of the world dulled, sound muffled, vision unfocused, and a screeching squeal

cut through me like the claws of a big cat. The cigarette tumbled down the front of my jacket, its cherry leaving dabs of ash in its wake, as I spun on my heels. My eyes took in every detail of every board sliding upward. My heart pounded with a stuttering jerk. I didn't want to look. My rational mind told me to expect a loose gutter, a swinging weather-vane dangling by a loose bolt, anything of a logic that some part of my mind already knew to be flawed.

No curtain swayed slowly in the aftermath of force, no vague shadow could be seen in the distance. No. Nature is never as subtle or tactful as that. Even with the glare of clouds across the glass, even with a cold, damp wind threatening to water my eyes, my sight was true. I could see it as well as I had ever seen anything. A figure on the other side of the glass. Tall and thin, so ungodly thin, and in dark, crisp silhouette. It swayed there, eyes stabbing through me. My breath was trapped mid-throat. Its slow swaying, so hypnotic, like a

metronome's last movements before suc-
cumbing to entropy. I couldn't break my
stare.

The whole of my mind was rapt with
the gravity of it. The immensity of the un-
believable. And at that moment I came
to a realization. I felt no fear. I could tell,
somewhere in my mind, that the eyes of
a hunter, that which I had felt so surely,
were not upon me. The gaze was not that
of palpable malice. Still, I needed tangible
proof to quell the nagging doubt that still
would not abide, a doubt that was strong
with a lifetime of enforcement as to what
could be. No matter how long I stared, and
that form stared back, the human mind
is capable of incredible amounts of ratio-
nalizing. It shifted quickly in its place and,
with an unearthly bend to its thin form,
dropped back from the window.

I hurried through as quickly as my
hobble would allow, the back door swinging in the breeze. A stack of papers fluttered in the wind that followed me through

the dining room. A bead of sweat trickled down my chest in a cold line. The front door was still fastened tight with the bolt, and a slow shuffle drifted from the back room. I didn't know what I was seeking or chasing. A muted thud came from upstairs as I crossed the room, and as I stopped at the foot of the stairs I was greeted by the billowing cascade of silence.

My foot pressed painfully against the edge of the step as I crept as quietly as I could up the stairs. The breath passing lightly through my nostrils sounded like the crashing waves of the beach. In the wavering gloom of a reinvigorated rain, my eyes passed over the little desk and chair and down the hall. A box of extension cords and pile of newspapers sat where they had sat before in the collective bedrooms, dust slowly growing to bury them with enough time.

Returning to my room, I found my sheets and blanket crumpled into a ball at the foot of the bed. While it had become

a mindless habit to make my bed since the time I had spent away, I imagined it wasn't outside the realm of possibility that I had forgotten that morning. I seemed to become more forgetful with each passing day. It was as I was just reaching for the pile when something caught my eye; something that cast away any notion of forgetfulness and solidified the great mystery that was already in motion, perhaps had been in motion for years.

The last drops were slowly dripping from the edge of the table, the puddle on the floor an ever-renewing bloom of rings from its center, my water glass from the night before on its side with a jagged crack running down its length. My body took a deep breath, independent of my mind, and in a moment so powerful that I could feel it being etched into the grooves, the smell raced to the forefront of my consciousness. It was fragrant and directed as a church censer. I turned my head toward the bed, my palsied hand hovering for a moment

over the pile of linen and wool.

I'm not sure what I expected to feel as my hand touched the fabric. Warmth? The moisture left when a person rises? Whatever it was, that was not what I found. It was cold, at least as cold as the room, if not colder, and as I pulled the bedding upward and revealed the taut bottom sheet, the fragrance was expelled in a great plume. Almonds.

That feeling was there, stronger than ever; one part felt that I should be afraid, probably more afraid than I had ever been before, but that another part of my mind knew better and that part was now in control. The piercing cry that I had heard, that swaying form. I didn't have a hunter eying me. I had a companion. Someone as trapped, as lonesome as I had felt, was also here.

I laid the pile as it had been on the bed and returned downstairs. Who is, or rather was, this person? Why were they trying to communicate with me? Most importantly,

why had it taken me so long to understand their objective?

From then on, I move the furniture with more care, as perhaps it had been theirs. In which case it still was. Who knew when I would be spied, moving something seemingly innocuous but perhaps the most important thing in their lives?

I worked slow, delicate lines sanding the floor. Each bowing board was no longer just lumber, but the history of human lives. I carefully cleared lines of compacted dirt from between the boards with my pocket knife; attentively worked old staples out of the wood or tapped detail nails back into place. I slid my palm over the wood, reveling in the velvety smooth of it.

That evening as I was having dinner in the living room, a thin coat of sawdust covering me, falling like snow when I moved my head too quickly, a rustling shuffle came from overhead.

"Seems like the rain's dying down," I said, twirling strands of ramen on my fork.

The strain in my muscles, the reworking of old fibers that had thought themselves to be long since retired, felt not like a burden but a rebirth. It wasn't work. It wasn't work on my house. It was the revitalization of these rooms for their true owner. That was the feeling that coursed through me as the sun rose and I had already been working on the floors for an hour.

The drips of sweat worked themselves into the boards as I slid the little sander along. Some new energy coursed through me, and I could feel my companion looking over my work. Swaths of bare wood grew with the pile of used squares of sandpaper and I lived as in a trance. My very thoughts were an endless stream that spoke with such conviction that I didn't notice the lack of inconsequential noises, the music, the television, that we usually demand in a home. The buzz of the sander became

background noise, and quickly nothing at all. I was one with my mind in a way that I hadn't been in a very long time.

I took breaks only for water, damn that eternal thirst, and welcomed the warm, sweet smell of lumber reopened to the world for the first time in decades. It was as though the fragrance had been brewing and perfecting itself for the day that it would be unleashed by some fine connoisseur. It was a resplendent intoxication that I could feel in my veins.

By three o'clock, the sun peeking through clouds with a little more vigor, I had a pile of beaten, purple paper free of sand and a level floor that you could have run bare nerves across without damage. I looked across my work, hands on my hips, and was given a brief moment of satisfaction, but as quickly as that contentment came I noticed the trim. It was as though my eyes were drawn to the sloppy work with mechanical force. Clumps of paint had dried dribbled and thick, or were so

thin that you could see the previous color beneath. After the care and love that I had put into the floors, the base molding was like a dollar store frame on a Van Gogh. Just an utter nullification of what my mind had envisioned.

I laid on my side, the final pack of sandpaper in the pocket of my sweatshirt, and started working my way around the room. The shoddy work of the white coat was a bit harder to work through, while the blue beneath slipped away with ease, exposing the lines of beautiful walnut that nearly shimmered in the light. The expert planing of the molding made quicker work of things than I had expected when, as I reached the final corner of the room, I saw a particularly ugly and clumped patch ahead.

I ran the first pass of the sander over the section. Though I had assumed it was globs of paint giving the effect, after a few moments I realized that the imperfections weren't due to an overabundance of paint but something below. The wood slowly

showed, first the grain as faint lines, then the color cutting through, but still, that odd configuration of imperfection remained. I would pull a few passes then blow upon it, then a few more.

Slowly the lines clarified to show intentional carving, then a bit more. Seemingly vague swipes became more determined. I watched as the ambiguity solidified into a concerted effort. As the wood became a backdrop, those lines of paint formed a message. In white, edged with a haze of blue, was the inscription 'ANNE V '92'. A thought clicked. I groaned as I rose after so much time laying on my side.

I dug through the pile of books, the light bulb casting an amorphous glow through collected dust. Eighty-five, eighty-seven, eighty-eight, ninety-one. As I dropped the book onto the pile at my side, it came into view. It was a burgundy yearbook with a large '92 embossed on the front, on the cover, in a clean blackletter was the name Holy Spring High School. I leafed through

the pages, slowing as I reached the V's at the end of each class, the children growing with each restart of the alphabet, and with each progression of age the thought that I had cracked some case dwindled. At the senior class, each student was given their own page. I flipped quickly to the end, Antonio Vante, Abraham Vaughn, Anne Vincent, Michael Voyles. Anne Vincent.

I'm not sure if it was true, or some hindsight projection, but I told myself that that was her, the girl from the dream. It would have made more sense, especially for those that don't have a daughter, if she had looked like Molly at all, but she didn't in the slightest. She was tall and brunette, where Molly was short with wavy, dirty-blonde hair (until she started dying it that is). There was a picture of her in a cheer-leading outfit, which seemed to be the one at the base of the stairs, though I couldn't be sure in black and white; another thing that was very far from anything having to do with Molly. She had some quote from

Tears in Heaven under her name, God how I have always hated that song. I'm guessing that's one thing that Molly and I would have agreed on musically.

They were probably as diametrically opposed as two people could be, but still, some part of my subconscious linked them. I suppose it was because that was around Molly's age when I had gone away. That I hadn't been able to be there for her turn to get those pictures taken, or to even know what color hair had been rendered black and white. Perhaps it's that I had some instinctive need to protect all of the girls that were an age that she had reached. Once you associate a daughter with an age, they all turn into your children. Where ideas come from, and how they contort before fruition, is a great mystery.

I stepped carefully over the uniform, tread up the worn steps, and turned off the light, the yearbook under my other arm.

The Shuffling Night

That night I dreamt of her again, but this time with the certitude that it was Anne. Her face was a clarity beyond reality, and with that clarity the personification of anxious dread. I rested my hand on her shoulder, but with each reassurance of safety, I was met with that same 'shh' from before. Cheeks and the tip of her nose went from healthy pink to the dull blue of cold death. A shadow settled over her face. The glint of her eyes was the only light to be found. Her arms crossed and gripped herself. In the vague darkness, her jaw descended, long, white teeth came into view, and I watched in horror as they came together in a violent chatter. Bits of enamel splintered away, blood trickled from gums lacerated by sharp points of tooth. The louder the chattering became the more blood gushed from her mouth. I could feel its cold flecks hitting my cheek.

I woke with a jolt that caught my breath in my throat. As the dream receded and reality took hold, something from that

other world remained. I could still hear it, that horrid chattering. It was coming from one of the back bedrooms, clearer than any of those benighted noises had been up until then. I laid with a long-dead stillness, not from fear for myself, but for fear of scaring her away. The tree branch shadows shook on the spot of illuminated ceiling above my head, and I watched their fearful tremors as her chattering died down. The wind rumbled a mournful tone against the walls, the shadows shifted with the wobbling pane of glass, and I heard the approach.

The swishing glide of cloth on weathered boards, as clear as the void of space, drew toward me from along the hall. I could feel the little beads of sweat develop and come together on my forehead, the fabric under my palms grow damp. Just keep calm, that's all that I had to do. I could see that gloomy hall from the corner of my eye and, though the sound was nearly upon me, not a shadow shifted or darkened patch

intensified. As the shuffling stopped at the foot of the bed a tinkling doubt wormed its way into my mind. How could I know what I was doing? No one would have known. What if I was wrong? I squeezed my eyes shut and pressed the thoughts from my mind. No! I was not going to push her away now, not when she was finally feeling comfortable enough to make her presence so clearly known.

My eyes shot open as I felt the bed shift. Not heard something from a different room, not smelled from the past, but felt, there and in the now. The legs creaked a low groan and the headboard tilted against the wall with a thud as pressure was applied to the foot of the bed. I slowly pressed myself up and onto a trebling elbow. My joints felt like jelly and weakness.

It was dark in the room but not too dark to see, with the whine of squeaking springs, the mattress beginning to sag by the pile of kicked-off blankets at the foot of the bed. The bloom of almonds in the

room was like I was drowning in them, so strong that I could feel the rich taste on my tongue when I opened my mouth.

"Hello, Anne," I said softly, and the sag of the mattress became more defined.

I pulled my feet back from the indentation. The sound of the wind, if there was any wind, was lost to me, how engrossed I was in the moment.

"I don't want you to be afraid," I said.

With that I felt the bed slowly draw back to its original place, the springs extended back to a flat surface, and the shuffling began again. The sound retreated back down the hall, my every instinct to attempt further contact, but logically knowing that I shouldn't push it. If there was a logic in that house. The sound muffled as she turned the corner, the room on the left I could tell from the sound traveling through the wall, and there was a dull thud, like a body falling to exhaustion.

The Shuffling Night

I descended the stairs, my eye aching from a nearly sleepless night of waiting and my body craving a cigarette. Thunder gave off a soft rumble from somewhere far off and I tried to process the events of the night before, to memorize the moments, the order, the every detail. I could tell that things were already starting to shift and distort, though I had spent the rest of the night replaying on loop. I dug through a drawer of the sideboard until I found the back of an old menu and stub of pencil that would do for recording.

"Just want to get everything right, so all of the details are there," I said with eyes tilted up. Its amazing how quickly it stopped feeling odd, talking to the aether.

After finishing with my record taking, I brewed a cup of coffee then stood in the dining room. The thought never even crossed my mind that I should go to the press, to try to milk any money or notoriety from the situation. This was a private matter. Instead, I grew further engrossed

in the room. With the warm beige of the walls, white trim just wouldn't stand out enough. There wasn't enough grandeur to it. My coffee was warming my mind, but I still found my right eye blinking excessively and my hand seemed drawn to rub.

I hurried along New Jersey Avenue, the umbrella in my hand closed but jerking in the gusting winds. The streets were vacant of life, and a twilight overcast was painted across the town. It seemed as though I was the only one heedless enough to stand up to the gods of weather. A grey cat, with matted fur and a chunk out of its ear, hopped down from the cemetery wall, gave me a quick look over, and slunk away under a car.

The hardware store was as desolate as the streets had been, and even the music seemed to have been set to a more sombre tone. There wasn't more time than to give a quick point from my eye to the kid, while

The Shuffling Night

I was walking down the aisle to the paint section. It was a smoldering anxiety to have the room finished flickering inside of me, like waiting for a delivery on a particularly good mail day. Depression seemed to be seeping through the large windows behind the owner at the register, that cold grey digging into dead fluorescent like a pile of leaches, and I was glad to have no one to wait in line behind and get out as soon as I could.

I pried the dusty lid of the can open with a rust-covered screwdriver, with little snowflakes of brown-red tumbling down into the lip. There was a clear divide where the paint had separated in the years that it had sat on the shelf, but its glorious richness could be seen through the yellowed translucence. My arm ached as I churned the stirrer in the can, a drop of sweat falling into the developing swirl before my arm could reach my brow.

Zachary Von Houser

With the edges all taped off, and a drop cloth to protect my work on the floors, I pulled long, slow strokes of burgundy over the wood. Raindrops knocked a cautious knock on the window and the trim gripped the paint without a grain to be shown. I took extra care in the last corner, making sure to use as little paint as possible and retain the white of the inscription. As I stepped back, it was a beacon of the past, something to remind those that came in who had been there before and to show Anne that she was still remembered. That combination of two simple words worked themselves over and over in my mind, 'show Anne', 'show Anne', until the idea came. The rain was manageable and I had a couple of hours to kill before I could seal the floor, so I could either do this or drink until then. With that justification, I went to the little convenience store downtown.

When I returned, I brought the yearbook upstairs and left it in a little patch of light on the floor, heedful to clear the spot of

dust before sitting it down. I tried reading some Baudelaire in the living room, but I could never make heads or tails of poetry.

I had read a lot of books during my time away, but for the most part all that was available were out-of-date school books for the guys trying for their GED's, (like that would do them any good with attempted murder on their background check) or the mass produced nonsense you would find on the shelves of a drug store, a thin layer of dust covering the top of their yellowing pages, infused with the smell of commercial cleaner and deodorizing spray until the next ice age. Someone had slipped an Edward Bunker book into the piled masses, but who wants to read about a hamburger when you were in the middle of being forced to eat three thousand six hundred and fifty hamburgers consecutively? Prison is prison, and the last thing that you want to break the monotony of it is to read stories about prison.

At the house, I had tossed aside any-

thing with the name Patterson, or Koontz, or Crichton, although I didn't really have a problem with Michael Crichton, it's just that his name is to be included in those drug store novels and if I'd read Androm-eda Strain once I'd read it thirty times. Underneath those, was a treasure trove of classics; for some reason in prison those were always the first to go when someone needed rolling papers, or to wipe their ass, or to set a little fire with a hidden match. Maybe its because even the dumbest of us had heard the titles enough times in school to make them commonplace, like there was some unstoppable factory pumping out one after another of the classics that they shoveled from a big pile into a truck and right over for us to wipe our dirty asses with and throw it at a guard.

Sitting in that quiet house, some of the greatest combinations of words, and thoughts, and feelings were all waiting for my every whim; so I switched back to Robinson Crusoe, the Wyeth painting on

the cover the beauty of a gem captured. Words sped by, gripping my consciousness in their tiger trap. My coffee cooled, the drone of traffic was a mantra in the back of my mind, and I was walking those beaches in the sun.

A soft knock from above brought me back to the living room. It was far from being late into the day, but at least three hours had passed since I had finished painting.

"Thanks for the reminder," I said.

The next two hours passed as if entranced, the soft, cool breeze coming in through the open window and that warm comfort of nearing the completion of a task that you felt a calling for. Golden rings shimmered through the sealant, an even higher level of vibrant glory against the deep red. I pulled the last stroke of my brush, crouching at the edge of the living room with a near-lithium contentedness, my hands speckled with polyurethane and feeling satisfyingly tender.

I finished the last sip of my beer, the can as speckled with sealant as I was, and turned to the living room for another. It took a moment before I stopped my spin and looked across the dining room into the kitchen. There on the table sat the remaining five of a six-pack.

The smell of hungry soil, chilled trees, and moisture that would have free dominion until spring hung in the air. I want to say that the season evokes some darling memories of candy apples and scarecrows with straw hands, but after a certain type of life, those memories are gone and all that your left with is a vague idea of forgotten joy. There's no mental home movies, not even a snapshot of time, just a hint of feeling, like your birth. And you take it, because it's better than the alternative.

I walked around the outside of the house, half-interestedly inspecting the siding planks; though they looked no worse than when I had moved in, they surely weren't going to get in any better

shape on their own. I rubbed at my eye, the flesh feeling bloated and firm, but not necessarily sore. Sprouts had sprung up between the gravel of the unused drive-way, marks of nature's occasional unpre-pared futility. As I rounded the corner and came to the back of the house, I gazed up at the window, hoping to catch another glimpse of her, no matter how brief. To my great disappointment, there was no motion to be found that day, only two cur-tained panes like a book left open for so long that its spine broke.

I stood in the center of the room looking over my work, a revitalization of old glory, a freeing of imprisoned great-ness. The shuffling overhead had become a constant, quickened scuffle for the last hour, and I took that as a grateful response to my efforts.

"Not too bad, is it?" I asked, raising my beer toward the ceiling. "I guess all of

those odd jobs finally paid off."

Though I had grown a warm comfort in this phantom company, it seemed a shame to do all of that work and not show it to anyone that would willingly, if not congratulate, then at least give a warm nod at the craftsmanship. I dug through a suitcase until I found my address book, still wary of my phone's ability to properly save a number in perpetuity. I had lost the right half of the cover some years before, and the pages turned against a crease as I flipped through them.

I slid along the yellowed pages, the line where my finger had run across that exact spot a thousand times before darkened with oils and worn ink. A lot of people my age joke about it, but it is a truly ghastly experience to realize how many of the numbers that you have saved are those of the dead. Logically, you should just cross out or tear the page of those departed, but something in your mind stops you. It's as though that number still being there is in

some way a connection to them nevertheless lasting, a final vestige of times in a fuller world.

With the list of those I would actually enjoy seeing being primarily composed of those in eternal rest, I was forced to be a bit less picky in my guest options. Somewhat firm acquaintances were quickly good enough, those faces that I had worked with and got along with a year or more ago were by default close chums for a lack of competition. I narrowed it down to eight, with a further two in case of unavailability. One nice thing if you're throwing a party after a certain point in life, if someone is without children or those children are old enough to fend for themselves, then you have very little competition on a Friday night. Twenty-four hours was an abundance of advanced invitation. It was forty-five minutes away, not across the country, after all.

I made a list after going through the kitchen inventory, looked out at the world of wet gloom beyond my window, and

felt the contrasting warm embrace of the house that much stronger. I could feel the rain drops waiting in the wings, priming themselves to soak into my bones. There was a reluctance in my muscles, like forcing yourself from bed after too-little sleep. A jagged rumble cut into the ambient shuffle as Anne moved some piece of furniture up-stairs.

"I need to go to the store," I said from the foot of the stairs, my voice forcing a sudden silence against the sounds of motion. "I shouldn't be too long." As much for her benefit, I was saying it to add a de-finitive point to my action. There would be no putting off once it had been said.

A feeling of foolishness pervaded as I pushed my little collapsible push-cart through the entrance. Everyone in the city seemed to have one of them in their basement or entryway, but here you would have thought that I was pushing a corpse

on roller skates along those treat-lined aisles. Eyes followed, and brows cocked like I was the most misguided rube the world had ever seen.

My wallet was a little light, so I had to be a bit more frugal than I would have liked to with certain things, but you have to know where to splurge and where to save occasionally. A slightly wilted head of lettuce, for a salad that most likely wouldn't even be touched, moved over a couple of dollars more for the roast; off-brand bullion cubes would add that little hint of flavor to potatoes just as well as the name brand. As I passed an endcap of reading glasses, rubber tips for canes, and sewing kits, I looked both ways before grabbing an eye patch.

I had just reached the checkout line when a waving arm caught my eye. Attached to the arm was an old woman, a desperate look of recognition contorting sagging flesh and weakened facial muscles. Someone pulled the cart up behind me,

and I was trapped. I noticed how one of her legs seemed to have some malady to it, some neurological or muscular lameness that gave her a hobbled gait. Her purple-grey hair gave me a slight flicker of remembrance, but it wasn't until she was nearly to me that I recognized her as the woman from the shop where I had bought Oscar.

It's terrible how some brief occurrence can give people cause to come up to you anywhere they please in public. She rambled and yammered, asking how Oscar was doing and describing in the utmost detail what new plants had arrived and all of their benefits to my life. I had never known that every plant on our planet has so many, most likely unverifiable, advantages, but it was apparently her mission in life to spread the good word. All that I could think of was home, around her droning blather; how I wouldn't have to speak to anyone about such mundane things, how I was never pressed into such

discomfort there. I was nearing the point where it seemed wise to just walk away from my cart and be done with this whole horrid situation once and for all, when the line moved forward and an end-cap of soda pressed a blessed divide between us.

A look of disbelief creased her brow, that I wouldn't willingly give up my place in line to continue our conversation, just before the Pepsi logo blocked her make-up-caked face. I doubt that I had said a single word in the whole exchange, though I would imagine it would have been one too many.

With everything put away, I pulled from the basement the pieces of furniture that seemed to need the least help in looking acceptable for the dining room. The table with with room to spare and, while it didn't perfectly match the side-board, chairs, or cabinet, I hoped that a tablecloth would hit its most blatant fea-

tures. Wood was dusted and oiled, cloth spot cleaned as well as I was able. By the end, the smell of lemon and dust seemed to have saturated my very essence.

I sat up in bed, a vigilance in my mind, but the pinprick of betrayal in my heart. I had almost immediately regretted my idea, but proof, not a trick of the mind, not tired synapses, was the only surety. Something that could be looked back at, at any time.

"It's not that I don't believe in you, it's just that I need something... tangible," I explained. "I've always been like that."

My shoulders were propped with pillows and my neck ached where my head was braced against the pitched ceiling. I took a small sip from the glass of water, wanting to give no in-way to any demands that would make me leave the bed that night, and tried to find a more comfortable position. Warm air crept up from the ground floor, but not to any extent that

saved me from having to pull the blanket up to my chest; a cold front had trampled in with the night, and with it the first warning jabs of a winter to come.

The floor looked like a barren field after a light snow, with gentle undulations rounded where the boards joined and mists of white rolling in the draft of the window. I could see the two cleared spots where my feet had stood, like lakes of black water that had refused to freeze. The flour bag sat beside the bed where I had dropped it, after scattering its contents across the floor and watching its sifting tendrils slide across the dry boards and up to the legs of my bed.

I could feel the wet cold of the draft, and briefly wished that I had closed the curtains, but the clarity of night between the parted and tied cloth was too glorious, the stars too bright and too many to be repressed. I considered staying awake, watching as the darkness deepened, fluctuating with its hinted shades of blues,

then purples, then the drowning richness of red as the sun threatened to break the night's grip on the land.

How would it be to see it all, to glance beyond the vale? If nothing else, if she was as elusive to the eye as she had been that night before, then I could at least be a beacon of comfort if I was to give attention. But what if I was wrong? What if my blatant wakefulness was an affront? What if the act of observation prevented the ability to show one's self?

The calculations were too complex, the rules too unknown. So, in the end, I tried to treat the night as I would any other night. I would close my eyes, take my mind to those far-off places that led me to sleep in the early days of having gone away, and let the blanket of night insulate me. To sleep was to not really be in a place, as what is to be in a place but to observe? If the mind is somewhere else, then the body might as well be.

The Shuffling Night

We strode through the mist, a slight breeze twirling it into whipping fins around my face. Questions popped into my mind, questions of every variety. Life and death, of the past and future. With every question thought, I would glance over, and a beatific serenity was so fully embedded into her face that I couldn't bear to break this uncommon peace.

My foot stumbled over something, a dampened snap reached me from below, and for the first time, I thought to look down. It wasn't the homogeneous white, that filling mist, as surrounded us from every other angle. I could still see the mist, though it split as though I were standing in a steady stream, and in the wake of my legs I could see ground. Not pristine, heavenly grass fields, nor spotless marble did we tread upon, but corruption. Rot we walked upon, like gods must feel around mortality. Spongy branches parted with slopping drips underfoot, rather than a clean snap; mosses pressed up water of a putrefied brown; soil that bubbled and brought death rather than life.

I stooped to pick up one of the sticks, and an iron grip clasped onto my upper arm. The cold seared my flesh. I could feel the tips of fingers threatening to puncture my skin where they met. I turned quickly and she was glancing down at me, head shaking slightly, her grip on my arm loosening.

"Shh," she said, and the mist began to take her.

My eyes felt gummy, as though they had been crusted with paste when I peeled them apart; my lungs burned dry and full of clots. I went to pull back my blankets, a ruffled cocoon that squeezed my chest, when a bubbling pain sprang from my arm. I touched the sleeve of my t-shirt with delicate fingers, a marrow-deep throb em-

anating, and peeled back the light fabric. A band of molted purple, like a faded funeral band, ran around my arm with capillaries, tributaries extending from some slaugh-ter-scene river, running outward.

What had I done to receive such pun-ishment? What infraction had ignorantly passed from me? I let the sleeve fall back across my arm and stretched muscles prodded by the rough spring bed. My mind felt slower than usual to adjust to the new day, which could account for how long it took me to process such a simple set of events. Either way, I suppose I had finally received the proof that I had asked for.

For a moment I thought that we were seeing the beginning of yet another day of gloom and grey, the room shrouded with a dull, suffering light, until I noticed the slight shadow of a flower flutter across the wall. The curtains swayed lazily, the two slowly deteriorating sheets of pat-terned fabric pinched tight together. At the bottom, the remains of one of the knit roses

dangled, its center torn free and what was left hanging by a thread.

I pulled away the blankets, which dragged heavy with sweat, swung my legs around, and nearly let them strike the floor before the thought clicked. I set my feet softly onto the heavy sheet of undisturbed flour below, the velvet softness enveloping my rough soles. Along the length of the bed, all was white and clear and smooth, but at the end, in that little gap between the wall and table, a strip of rich wood shone through clear. Little waves of white cascaded outward from my footfalls. At the foot of the bed, running from the stairs, across and into the hall, not a speck of flour, dust, or anything else littered the floor. I didn't even have a moment of question, because a hundred movies rushed to mind. Of course, the floor was clear of dust. It must have been the gown. Ghosts always wear long, flowing gowns, don't they?

The Shuffling Night

The leaves on one snapped off branch had browned incredibly fast. I would have imagined that it would take at least a day or two, but it couldn't have been more than nine or ten hours. After scraping that last bits of soil from the floor and replacing them in the pot, I adjusted Oscar so that the snapped bit of remaining branch wasn't the first thing that I saw. Every day, there was some new ailment that seemed to be wreaking havoc upon him, but ailments wouldn't have shoved him from the table. Even little clusters of leaves had browned far from the broken branch, their dried cells crumbling with the slightest breath. The brown leaves ran in four stripes, like the stripes of brushed fingers. Ailments wouldn't have pushed him from the table, but something must have.

I went through the drawers of the sideboard, pulling sheet after sheet of delicate fabric, worried that even the slightest twitch would send their fragile filaments to shreds. I placed the pre-industrial doilies

at a measured distance from the lamp on the sideboard and beneath the ashtray in the living room, backing up from each to ensure their precision. Heavy creases and lines of yellow age ran through the table cloth. I had little time or ability to do anything about the color, but the creases I could work at. I rubbed the thick eye patch before going for the iron.

The water splashed cold into my pint glass, filling it as near to halfway as I could manage, then the pink tentacles spread and spun and dissolved as the flowing Bordeaux brought it up to the top. I know, it was still a bit early to start drinking, but it's bad luck to cook without a glass of wine. Besides, there was water in it.

I took a sip that drank down a third of the pint, checked the temperature of the oven, and slid in the roast. A pile of vegetables sat on the rough wooden table, cornucopia-like in the sharp light of the crisp, clear day. The swinging tail of the cat clock happened to catch my eye, and I noticed

that I was already running behind; it was only by twenty minutes, but on such a day noting but precision would do.

Out of the shower, a tan smear from the work and a few days of neglect in showering running to the drain, I pulled my suit from the closet across from the stairs leading up to my room. The plastic smell of the vacuum bags permeated the fabric, and I sprayed it down heavily with Polo before pulling on my slacks. Still, I could have sworn I could feel the tingle of chemicals on my skin. I straightened my suspenders as I pulled them over my shoulders, tucking my shirt taut beneath. I pinched the dimple on my tie as I dragged the Double Windsor snug, I'll never understand how fully grown folks could think a single looks good. Another fifteen minutes to get ready, and all that I had to do was put on shoes.

At the foot of the stairs, I heard the creak of my bedsprings and decided it would be best to wait. I would give her

her time to do whatever she felt driven to do. It was just as much her place as mine, perhaps more so if you took into account the amount of time she had spent. There was a rattle of the bed frame, the merest whisper of a tread, and a soft shuffling away from the stairs and my room.

I stood on the penultimate step, leaned across, and grabbed my shoes. A thin coating of flour sprinkled the patent leather, across which I blew and the brushed clear. While I tied my shoes, I notices two new lines of flour had been cleared from the floor. I stepped over to the window and let the fragrance envelop me. The almond was utter relaxation, a release of the weight of the bricks that piled onto my back year by year. It drifted and was drawn to me, and I let it come, myself drifting into a sea of better calm than humanity had ever known. The very rim of the sun clung to the upper edge of

The Shuffling Night

the window, glinting a warm wink onto my skin. The trees waved a good-bye to me that I could see, even when my eyelids had settled closed.

I felt a warmth and comfort that I was helpless to resist. It was as though I was aware of nothing, and yet aware of the feel of every board, every fiber, every atom around me; I could feel their hum, the slight sinking of the walls, the floors into rest. I counted and savored every breath.

Something must have been wrong with my count, or the time between each, because the knock that brought me to also brought the smell of the roast well along toward completion. The sun bobbed, low and burdensome just above the roof of the accountant's. Still, I stood there watching until another pounding of the door coerced me into shaking my head clear.

John stood at the door, his hair a grey hood over a face prematurely wrinkled

from too many years of working at the same smoky bar. He had decided to grow a mustache at some point since I had seen him last, which wasn't alleviating the faux-years that had etched themselves into him. The sparkle that seemed to dart about in his eye was still glaring strong, the last remnant of a youthful ambition for life. The richness of the golden-hour backdrop made him look that much more muted in comparison, like some stage prop corpse.

I stood, unsure where to go from there, until he asked, "So, can I come in?"

"Oh, yeah. Sorry."

I showed him the chair that I had set aside for coats, quickly cut through the dining room, and into the kitchen. I would wait on the tour until everyone else had arrived. That is if they even would. I had been having a problem with my memory recently, and couldn't be positive who had and hadn't confirmed. I'm not even sure if I could say that I was absolutely positive who I had actually gotten a hold of. Just to

have another person, someone that I could see and touch and have a conversation with, inside the house with me made my cheeks feel warm; the feeling like embarrassment or a fever. The thoughts were a little foggy.

He tended a bar down the street from that last place that I had worked in the city, the type of place where you only ordered a draft when you were completely certain that the lines had recently been cleared and you only went between the hours of five and ten. Any earlier and you would certainly run into the old drunks whose beers filled more quickly with tears and they could put them down. Any later and you were falling into shoulder-to-shoulder volume between the art school chic that couldn't wait to tell their other trust-fund cohorts about the new shit-hole that they had found, and the locals who were all too happy to be the center of this zoo-visit popularity. John was a good guy though. He remembered my drink from the first day on,

always kept the greedy hoards from a recently vacated seat for me, and was a gem at trivia knowledge from years of Jeopardy playing in the background of the bar. You always kept talking to a minimum during Jeopardy. God save the poor soul that attempted to put a dollar in the jukebox.

John helped himself to the refrigerator and opened us each a nice pumpkin ale that I had managed to find in the heart of bathwater suburbia. It felt a bit early for me, but to spend time with John without a drink seemed a strange sense of sacrilege. The roast was coming along well, and he pushed the pile of vegetables back on the table so there would be room for our drinks. In the moments after I had shut the oven door, as we stood at opposite ends of the kitchen, I couldn't point to a single moment where we had been alone to talk, let alone sober and in the light of even a dying sun. You see, while I occasionally spent time at his work, most of our encounters were at the after-hours. During

those too-late ventures, there had always been a buffer, some chatty catalyst to move the conversation along. We were each pinpoint highlights to the meal of talk, not the main bulk. Worst came to worst, there was always someone streaming in from work with a grievance to entertain us with. As the host, I felt the burden of taking up that post as speaker, but small talk doesn't work when you've had countless drunken remorses spilled in the past, and deep conversation is a nonstarter when most of the foundations were lost to the alcoholic abyss.

The moments were getting a little edgy when a loud knock at the door pushed a breath of air into my lungs.

"Thank fuck," I muttered as I sat my beer down and gestured that I was going to see who it was.

I could hear the scattered voices before I made it to the living room.

"She did not say that!" Lauren's voice cut through the glass.

"Dear, I am *absolutely* sure that she did. *Absolutely*."

Lauren was turned toward the back of the quartet when I opened the door. Her perfume jabbed at me like a puff of razors and the fur on her faux-leopard coat seemed to be going through mange. The mud water tan of her roots was beginning to show through the red-blonde that didn't go with her complexion at all. I couldn't stand Lauren. Unfortunately for me, I liked Evan, and never betwixt the two could anything come. So, if you wanted to see Evan, the other eye would always see her.

"You are so full of it, Billy," she turned on heels that seemed beyond her skill-set. "Hello, darling!"

"Come on in, folks. Welcome to the new abode."

Lauren kissed my cheek, and I knew that it would stink of her for the rest of the night. Evan had a leather jacket over two arms tattooed with Japanese sleeves, which I thought were kind of funny for a

The Shuffling Night

Polack from Maine, but who am I to judge? I've got a surfboard on my chest with 'hang ten' beneath it. Know how often I hang ten? Never. I never hang ten.

"How's it going, man?" Evan asked, and gave me a one-armed pat as he passed, in his other hand was a bottle of Heaven Hill and a plastic bag of miscellaneous beers.

"Hey!" Travis said, in the slightly uncomfortable way that he always spoke at parties, but in that endearingly uncomfortable way. He always put a hand out, like he expected a handshake, and then gave you a full hug.

"Let me get some of that love," Billy pushed between and embraced me. "Permission to come aboard, captain?"

"Permission granted," I said, readjusting my eye patch slightly.

There was something about Billy, I'm not sure if it's the nineties haircut that he held like a war relic or the alarming disparity between age and dress, that always made him look like a little kid. I have no

idea how, in twenty years, Travis hadn't dropped him into a box in the night and mailed him across the world.

"If she had said that, and I'm *not* sure she had, then why did I see her with him Saturday night?" Lauren jumped back in as soon as they cleared the threshold.

"Well, then why don't you ask Tonya--" Billy started.

"Oh, now you expect me to believe Tonya? Jesus, I might as well believe you..."

A party is easier than a conversation, because the obligation is gone. You don't have to constantly be *on*. You can join into a conversation, and when the subject gets too dull, or annoying, or deep for the mood that you're trying to keep, then off you go to check on something, or just quietly step away and you have a moment to breathe. The only downside is when you haven't been around people for an extended period of time, the mere energy of

amassed human personalities can catch in your throat and you end up stepping away more often than staying in place. I had just made such a move when I saw Evan in the kitchen, staring absentmindedly at the oven. I think anyone who cooks for a living gravitates toward kitchens, like a dog to his kennel, because at least it's an understandable madness.

"Prime rib," I said.

"I took a peek, looks pretty."

I'd seen him with everything from a shaved head to it falling down at his shoulders. At the moment he had something Hitler Youth adjacent and kept patting down a cowlick in the back.

I pulled the roast out slightly, to give that trite approximation of bragging that happens in the kitchen, peeled back a corner of foil, and spooned over the jus; the onions, carrots, and meat melding into a smell that took me back somewhere from a long time before.

"Got quite a nice little place here," Evan

said.

"Beats sharing a studio with a bunch of rats and roaches."

"Yeah, that place above the Chinese joint was pretty fucked."

A light thud came from above, imperceptible unless you had come to know the variety of sounds that emanated in that house very well.

"Want to help me set the table?" I asked when I was confident that it was one of her singular sounds and not the start of a continued commotion.

"Sure."

Lauren was talking to Billy in the living room, her voice a high squeal in times of excitement that cut through the music I had playing. Travis gazed at one of the old paintings that hung on the other side of the room, while John pushed around through the bowl of mixed nuts that I had put on the sideboard.

The Shuffling Night

The clatter of forks and knives on the old basement-china was a blessing. A quiet had fallen over the group, eyes downcast at plates or reaching for serving spoons and, while the food was good, it wasn't that good. I surveyed the faces around the table, without too heavy an amount of blatancy, and really envied Jesus. At least he didn't have to look his buddies in the eye when his last party went south. When I looked over and saw that even Lauren hadn't the slightest of interest in talking a chill went down my spine. Yes, I'll admit that a rumbling avalanche of anxiety had crashed over me at the start, but to be seen as some party leper was an equal curse. I was already miles from everyone that I knew, pacing hollow halls in isolation, and to not even be able to bring this group back for another visit, to be cast out in totality, was oblivion.

"I think this place might be haunted," I regretted saying as it passed my lips.

"Ooo, how fun!" Lauren let the food fall

from her fork.

"I don't like any of that scary stuff," Billy said.

"I noticed the couch floating across the room, but I didn't want to say anything and embarrass you," Travis said.

"Seriously," I said, and gave a brief recap of what I had experienced thus far, of course leaving out the more emotionally charged elements. To be thought of as some *believer was one thing, but I wouldn't let them into the part that was mine. To them, I was just an objective observer.*

As I finished, Lauren said, "I could have told you that. You know that I'm a medium."

"I would have taken you for a small," Billy said, but no one was giving him the attention demanded.

"Quiet you old bitch, I am. My grandmom also had the second sight and saw it in me since I was a little girl."

"Alright--" Evan started.

"*You* might not believe in it, *you* never believe in anything besides your work, but

our kind host obviously does. So, as I was saying, we should have a seance. Then we can hear what this *Anne* thinks about everything."

The dishes were cleared away, which elicited a frown and sigh from Evan, who had yet to finish his potatoes. Candles were placed in the center of the table, and the lights were killed. Only the fervent flickering illuminated in orange spots on the eyes of the guests, sat equidistant from each other. The cold air pressed in on the walls like blocks of lead. The wind picked up and gave a rumbling shove against the windows, which I had to admit aided in the ambiance.

As Billy gripped my hand in clammy softness, and John sat his beside mine, the rolling weight of some treachery came to a scratching rest in my chest. It was a trust that I was bestowed with and had broken, for what? To stop a moment's quiet?

A pinpoint of clarity showed me as a man weaker than I had thought. I just

hoped that the time spent in the beyond had left her more forgiving than I was feeling toward myself; but, as with most things hoped for, those are the very aspects slashed to the soil.

"Oh, great spirits!" Lauren tilted her head back. "We come in hopes to make contact with your great side of existence."

Evan gave a quiet giggle, and her closed eyes squeezed tighter. The candle in front of me swirled lightly against its tether. I'm not sure if anyone else noticed, but the flickering dance cut into me as a sign.

"Our friend, the man whom you share this house with, has told us of your willing-ness to communicate with the living, and we want you to know that we mean you no harm. Ours is a quest for knowledge, not to cast you from your rightful home. So please great spirits, I beg you, to give us a sign if you are there!"

I felt the pressure shift against my eye

beneath the patch, squeezing it shut for some alleviation.

"Any sign, dear spirits! Please, do what you can!"

I could feel Billy's hand growing damper against mine. Rain pelted the window in a decaying marching beat. The flames whipped their passions against the air. The setting was right, all of the choreography was there, so if there was going to be a time, that would be it.

Nothing. Not so much as a nervous knee making a glass shake. Just dull, dead air. Like most of the events that shape the foundations of our lives, timing glides the slightest of things into an unalterable order.

Evan's cackle broke the silence. Two of the candles went out in the motion of the table, as everyone besides Lauren fell into an uproar that blotted out the thudding rains.

Travis licked his fingers and pinched the flames from the candles, cutting the

light from the room, giving the slightest hope for a somewhat spooky moment, until John turned on the overheads. There was everyone, electricity the antithesis of that Victorian wonderworld that had been hoped for.

"I'm going to grab a smoke," I said to the crowd quickly dispersing from the dining room.

No remonstrations met my statement, so I grabbed my cigarettes from the sideboard. I'd had enough drinks to be interested in my own interests. I went out the back door, the edge of the top step crumbling under my foot. Raindrops were few and far between, but when they hit they were big and heavy. I stumbled down the steps, my thoughts a hazy fog of propensity.

Every inch of ivy growing clumped on the wall seemed the most important thing to me. I studied their leaves as I ran my eyes ever upward. Perhaps that floral interest was a shaky guise, that my mind

had set its aim of focus, but didn't trust me to follow through. The ivy drew me along its near-black leaves, each an arrow to the next. I knew what I longed to see at the mount, but could never admit to it.

A smiling, understanding face, commending me for my actions, glad to have a gathering of company brought into the fold. A child in need of that communal affection for so long. In the Good Book days, I suppose this would have been the time for smiting, for the great, gathering bolt to cut down, or lame, or enplague me, but my mystical guide wasn't one for the theatrics of an early-days god. The curtains sat still as a painting on the glass.

Upon opening the kitchen door, the pressure in my eye bloomed, as though I had just opened the hatch to some high-flying plane. It throbbed with the beat of my heart, and I was certain that if I slid my finger under the fabric patch and pressed the tender flesh, the pulse would be stronger than that in my chest.

I passed along the stove, my thoughts so intently set on the throbbing blind eye that the other was focused somewhere a thousand miles away. The depths of the discomfort made my stomach feel as though it was filled with the same putrefaction that I could imagine swelled above my cheekbone. A warm hand fell to my forearm, and the jostling combination of worlds external and internal swirled in my mind for a moment.

"So, do you honestly believe in all of that spook-show charlatanism?" The corners of Travis' mouth twitched upward, as they were often to do in a concentrated moment of bewildered amusement.

"It's just..." The pressured mass shifted under my skin. "Just some fun."

"I mean, I could see some of these people falling for the hokum mystics." The warning, like that of a broken bone before the pain, pushed freezer-cold sweat up

from my pores. "...you I couldn't see."

The hardened blobs of paint on the cellar door seemed to bulge and palpitate.

"Of course not." I sputtered blindly.

A confused crease spread over Travis' forehead.

"If you'll... I'll be right back."

Five degrees dropped as I shut the door to the cellar-way. The yellow-hued bulb swayed a coat of jaundice across everything in its proximity. At the foot of the stairs, a sea of darkness. The molt-filled silver of the mirror on the back of the door threw back my reflection in pestilence patterns. My face lived behind the speckling of dust like a worm-riddled woodcut. I ran my finger across the edge of the eye patch, a curtain sparing the mind of the horrors that befell flesh.

I slowly slid the patch back, feeling every fiber slip past over-sensitive nerves. Every hue, from flesh, to red, to purple, was half blended across the skin. The lower eyelid, at its most aggressive near to

the tear duct, was swelled nearly to closed. I watched my heart beat in that little spot of tear-making innards.

I pressed my finger lightly from the outer corner of my eye inward. Little slices of skin pulled too-tight ran down onto my cheek. As I neared the center, I saw a small white dot appear on my duct. So, there was the cause of all of my discomfort? I held tight the pressure of one finger and brought the other just below the duct. The mass, that great bunch of awful, slid and squirmed under my touch. With a hesitance that knew disgust to come, I slowly pressed the fingers together. The pressure built, cold and hot. Sweat popped from pores. I felt a slippery eel of bile squirming upward through my organs. Something like a rip that you can't actually feel, but know just the same, hammered at the duct. My knee wobbled. And suddenly, release.

A string of white squirmed from the duct and onto my finger. A noise came from somewhere. I pressed harder, and the rush

of a thousand hurried bristles came from within as the strand struggled outward. Not a sound of the party. Of the thousand sounds that a party is apt to make, there are some that it isn't. The evacuation eased the pressure on my eye and that of my mind. It was then that I could actually hear, and take in, the noise. A slow sifting was coming from below and to my left. The end of the pale strand fell onto my finger, the pressure eased, and I was free to look.

I breathed deep, and brought my thumb toward my finger, ready to smudge the physical manifestation of my discomfort from existence forever, when the sifting at the foot of the stairs turned to a frantic rustle. I flicked on the light, its exuberance struggling before finding its footing.

The cheerleading outfit bustled and writhed in jagged jerks upon the trash bag. A sleeve fell out across the plastic, looking for form.

"...said it was upstairs," a feminine voice said from the other side of the door. I

jerked a look at the door when movement on my finger shocked me from the reverie.

Nearly transparent appendages unfurled from the strand of white. The motion on the trash bag grew to a thrashing madness. The thing slipped in its steps of early life across my finger. A nausea that I had never known, which I know every moment of these days past, lurched in my stomach. I saw the thing flail on the tip of my finger. I can only imagine it was its head in a bedlam whip in the air. Its legs stumbled while I was in an awe of disgust. Its slithering form fell through the air. A quivering revulsion shivered over my skin. I gazed at its terrible, as it squirmed on the rough pine board at my feet. That had been inside of me, that manifestation of loathing. In a moment of repugnance beyond repugnance, I pressed the sole of my shoe into its butter-soft form. I think that I heard a shriek from the base of the stairs, but that could just be the fate of my life pressing inward.

"...okay?" I heard from the other side of the door.

"I'm fine!" I said.

I heard, through those thankfully thin walls, talk of going upstairs in a joking tone. Their steps worked their way around the stairwell, from what would have been the dining room, to the living room, and into the room at the stairs to the second floor. I rushed out of the stairwell, through the rooms, the cold gripping my sweaty flesh. I caught them just ascending the stairs.

"Don't go up there," I sputtered.

"Are you alright?" John asked.

I saw myself in the window, the sweat and paleness clear in the reflection.

"Yeah, I'm fine," I said, and proceeded to give a vague reason of electrical problems as to why they shouldn't go up.

I thought to myself that I never should have brought it up. I never should have betrayed such a trust.

"Sorry guys, I'm just not feeling great... too many drinks. You know," I forced out,

as I moved them toward the door.

The leaves shivered at the edge of the walkway, and a cold wind of smoke and rot pummeled along the road.

"If, you know, you need anything, just give me a call," John said, at the end of the group heading down the walkway.

"Oh, yeah. Definitely."

I could feel the tension swing over my head as the door shut. There was a vengeance to the house. I walked, head hanging, to the top of the cellar stairs. The uniform hung slack, the streak of white still lightened the top of the stairs.

A slam of some massive weight came from overhead, chips of mold-backed paint tumbled from the slanted ceiling beneath the stairs to the second floor. I hurried with the panic of a parent to their screaming child. Slam. The banister gripped my sweating palm. Slam.

At the top of the steps, wind buffeted

136

rain against the window with set drops glowing like little explosions from the light beyond. The storm-battered roof threw the atmosphere into a world of hissing static.

The room was in turmoil. The bed pulled from the wall, the table knocked over, the top of the desk at the far side a broken, jagged valley in the dimness. Sheets and knickknacks scattered the floor at my feet. A softer thud called to me from the end of the tenebrous hall. Thunder cracked from somewhere far enough that the accompanying light never graced my flesh.

The room looked much as it had. Vacant, forgotten, and lost.

"I'm sorry that I told them about you," I said. "Sorry that I brought them into your house."

A squirming ball of remorse tumbled within the tender sides of my guts. I knelt and touched the cover of the yearbook, the grooves of the pressed seal like some mystical sigil under my finger.

Zachary Von Houser

A light thump came from the dark corner across the room. The clip of my dress shoes echoed in the multi-angled room, all hardwood and wood panel. I pulled my hand up to the side of my face to block the struggling light that came through the thin window and the corner slowly grew clear. A crumpled sheet of newspaper, a couple of mismatched buttons, and bare floor.

Surprisingly bare floor.

I crouched and ran my fingers across the boards. Bringing them closer, I saw just how clean my fingertips were. Throughout the rest of the room, the floor had a coat of yellowed dust, but not on this thin strip. This strip that ran right to the wall.

I lightly pressed my ear to the panel, though I expected to hear only rain as by all accounts I had always presumed the wall to be external. Ever so softly, the tender hiss of shuffling steps came to me. In the unlikely attempt to hear something more, though I knew not what, I pressed the slightest bit more. It was then that, in

that dark vacant room, of the cold, barren house, the wall retreated with an equaled speed.

I dropped back from where I crouched and extended my hand. The panel was warm where my face had leaned. I shoved and the wall pushed away, swinging back and away and back, like a corpse at the end of the noose or a bladed pendulum, until it came to rest once more. Hidden away at about hip height, a hinge had been built into the wall and I had to crawl forward as I pushed once more and peered into the gloom.

The smell of mildew, forgotten lumber, and almonds as thick as cobwebs filled the room. Though I couldn't see the source, a feeble light granted me some tenuous illumination. Just enough to make out the mass laid out against the wall across from me. I could see the cloth, the faintest subtleties of former colors fighting to be seen through the dust; a pink or orange here, perhaps a shade of green there. Could this

be the reason why she had come to me? Could this be the one thing keeping her from peace? That she needed someone to find where she had laid for the final time?

The door swung shut behind me and an inch of dust pressed up and over the space between my sliding fingers. I had to stay hunched beneath the low, pitched ceiling of the tiny room.

The light and sounds of the street snuck in, bars of measured reality granted entry between slats of wood running across an arched window filling most of the opposite wall. In a deeper darkness, in the corner to the side of where I had entered, a pile of shredded newspapers lay next to a fat coil, like a massive hose. I was in the gabled dormer that pointed skyward above the front door, a place so obvious that I had never wondered about its location from inside.

The sleeve of a sweater extended across the floor from the mass of cloth, piles of dust like cotton batting collected

140

in the folds of material.

I shook away a light fog that was sifting into my mind. I wouldn't be a coward again. Wouldn't balk when action was demanded. There must have been something there that she needed me to see. Why else would she have brought me there? The tides of history, even just within the confines of my own mind, wouldn't be inscribed with an unwillingness to help the helpless. My feet moved with a surety without waver.

The sweater shifted as I stood above it, the insignia of the school rising and falling softly but irregularly. My knee cracked as I knelt. The rain splattered little droplets through the slats in the window and the mouldering, motionless air fought against the cleanliness beyond. I knew that I would feel the thin, hard structure of the ever-lasting remnants of death, that I would be touching that which once was. I watched more than considered as my hand came to rest softly on the cloth.

A terror rocked through me as I felt

it, a wriggle in a way that no earthly thing should, jagged bits vying to pierce my palm where they had no right to be. It was then that I noticed those other things beside the sweater; though less ghastly, their collection was no less horrid. A balled-up towel where I had presumed a shirt, torn bits of old, soiled rags where I had guessed a clump of eternal raven hair would have been.

I shouldn't have seen. No mortal eyes should see. But I had to see, had to know, what moved beneath that aged wool.

My fingers gripped the emblem with as much pressure as their trembling numbness would convey. A slipping and sliding tingled across the nerves of my oversensitive flesh. I swallowed, though my mouth was coated in an arid paste. I knew that I hadn't the fortitude for caution, that the only way I could endure to see would be all at once.

The sweater flew away in one swift blur. Dust snowed down around me. A des-

iccated tomb of minuscule bones lay in a grisly pile. Hundreds of ribs and skulls of every small animal imaginable intertwined. Shattered femurs pointed from enlarged eye sockets, the paper-thin structures of wings were crumbled shards. Through it all, movement abounded.

Long, thin, pale bodies. Multitudes of legs attached to slithering forms climbed through fleshless mouths, squirmed around barely-holding chains of vertebra. Damp antennae twitched at the head of engorged bodies in their movements through that monument of death. All repulsive, all loathsome, all a madness-propelling enlarged version of that thing that had pressed out of my eye.

I thought that I could handle no more, that I could endure not another thing without falling into an unsummitable pit of disgust.

A noise, like the sharp clacking of nails, called out from the darker corner, where bright light had likely not graced since the

last roof-board had been hammered into place.

My vision blurred for the first instant that it emerged from the shadows. That tube of body, as thick as my waist, uncoiling from the dark. From bulge-laden segments of sickly blue-hinting white, a hundred decrepit legs pulled it along. Bulbous knobs of festering fissures seeped from various spots on the sections. The final segments of its ten feet of length dragged behind with broken, dead legs. Through the grace of something greater, I could see vividly only in the stripes of streetlight that glowed on the floor, but those moments bore a shattered wasteland of mind. The slow *shh* of its dragging body overpowered in such close confines, with some liquid putrescence glinting in its wake.

I took a single step back, desperate to be as far as possible from that desecration-borne thing, and its almond stench. It was then that the reality of it all sank in. Every remembered second of Anne

changed, looking at her hideous glory. Those moments smashed into my mind, the false thoughts, the sinking of the bed, so much time lost in my mind, lost synapses of compassion. To know that they were caused by a thing of such mind-bending repulsion. The truth of those moments clattered upon me like a pile of jagged glass. The words of gentle consolation. The night in bed, to have been in such close proximity of that abomination; to picture its form slowly pulling down springs.

It slinked forward, its jagged legs catching on a segment of the deeply-gouged wall, and dragged itself upward, upward. Its slipping legs let out a nauseating screech. It was that noise that forced me into reality and to retreat back once more.

I'm unsure what I did to draw its attention. My mind fought to keep hold of the moment, to not be lost in some dream that came with the wafting smell. What was different than any other motion in those endlessly stretched seconds? I suppose

the favor of the gods is a fleeting thing, because it suddenly stopped in its ascent and landed with a shattering thud.

The jaws of that great grotesquery, how they chattered as it turned its head toward me; rough bone scythes slipping sharply across each other and stopping only when they crashed into what I can only describe as tumorous bulbed protrusions. The inner parts of that wretched, gaping maw, how glad that I could only vaguely take in their unspeakable workings.

My back pressed against the window slats, my hands pressed back and grabbed the rotting, spongy strips of wood, oily liquid running across my skin. It turned toward me, that face, an obsidian dome split vertically with a jagged rut. The two plates at either side stared with an alien blankness that bled an indifferent malignancy. Its jaws clattered and head bobbed, locked onto my intrusion. The long body, the color of pale rot, blocked the only exit.

It took a step toward me. Shh. My teeth

clamped down on tongue. Shh. I then did the hardest thing that I've ever had to. I took three long steps forward, somehow forcing myself closer even as it began its horrid march toward me. Shh. Viscous liquid squirmed from the open recess between mandibles, the stench came off of it cold. Still, I couldn't force myself to do what I knew I must.

I could see swirls of rotted green across the segment behind its head. Only two boards separated us. What could a probable death hold against the certain, especially when the certain came with such slow deliberateness? A calm fell over me. One board. With the last bit of control that I held over a world that had seemed determined to crush me down at every corner, that last option we are all born with, I rushed back with any bit of force left within me.

The slats broke around me like rotten, sopping death itself. Bits of damp, pulpy wood clung to my flesh and clothes. I felt

the fresh air blowing across me. I saw the lawn below as my head tilted down, heels rose up. The rain washed the anxiety, the floating death of that room, the visions etched into my eyes away. I was fine with the end, so long as I wouldn't end up a part of that desecrated nest of death, feeding the young of that thing, within that tomb of a house. A death out of walls, outside of the entrapments of the world. That was a death I could be happy with. All of that motion of half a second, as my shoes passed the drooping bits of slats, and it stopped.

My body struck the house with a sickening crack of ribs and the air left my body for what seemed the last time. Then I was rising, exhaustingly slowly, but I was rising. My shin ran and ground against the still-firm window frame. The slats of cedar siding scrolled across my vision and my fingers gripped weakly at each lip of them. Pressure built as my knee neared the window, nearly bending itself back-

ward, until some automatic jerk of my body turned me to my side. My calf cleared the windowsill, with a hissing tear from my pants, then the start of my thigh. Then I realized that I was being dragged back into that den of desolation by my cuff, brought as a feast for this thing's abominable children.

I pushed my arm out straight, catching the side of the window frame. The force was unbearable. My elbow burned, then screamed; the knotted ball of my hip, forever sliding easily within its joint, was slowly pulled toward the edge of its socket. I dug my nails into the peeling red paint of the window trim. The pressure rose in my cheeks, in the back of my eyes. My foot pulled the slightest bit from my ankle with a tumbling grind of little bones. The skittering slip of a plethora of clawed legs slid across the floor. My fingernails started a slow peel from their beds. A vacuous pressure built in my hip and I heard a tearing that I thought could only be the ripping of

tendons.

Then I was falling. Head over foot, The sky, the trees, the lawn, the sky, the trees, the lawn, the ever-present force of gravity pulling at my guts.

I hit the lawn with a sickening thud, only worsened as my knee snapped against the decorative bricks that lined the walkway. I stared up at the house, the rain splattering across my face, a faint hint of the full moon peeking through clouds at the tip of the gable. It was there, broken, exhausted, unwilling of spirit, that I saw it, my Anne in her horrid true form, crawl from the broken slats of the window and onto the roof. I felt those large, dead eyes watching me from the gable. I still feel them now, when I can't see out through a window, into those dark nights. There must be some power watching over me, no matter how spiteful, because I passed out there.

150

The Shuffling Night

It turns out Anne Vincent was alive and well, according to research, but my daughter, I couldn't find her anywhere online. I suppose you can't find anyone that doesn't want to be found by you. Perhaps she'll decide to contact me someday. If not I understand that some things aren't worth finding. Sometimes you get a strawberry, sometimes a lemon, and sometimes you don't know which would have been better.

THE END

www.ingramcontent.com/pod-product-compliance
Lightning Source LLC
Chambersburg PA
CBHW032019150726
47990CB00005B/2044

THE
LONG
SHIFT

OFF SOUTH PRESS

ISBN 979-8-9851855-0-8

9 798985 185508 >

Also by Zachary Von Houser

Dreams of the Dead Night

THE
LONG
SHIFT

ISBN: 979-8-9851855-0-8

Front cover image by Zack Traum
Book design by Zack Traum

First printing edition 2021.

Off South Press

For Cacey
umqua

The Long Shift

Nothing stirred on the fourth floor, not even the drywall dust that coated the floors and walls and every adornment that had welcomed the thousands that passed down those, now quiet, halls. The smell of sweat and coffee and stale smoke lingered, a permanent impression hovering in place for the next welcome draft. Drywall, scaffolding, tools, and discarded paper cups were piled against the door to the eastern stairwell, safeguard-

ing supplies against the maleficent plans of those who wished for an easier score of money. A pile of ash and cigarette butts coated the top of the sand-filled bucket by the window, with the rays of light reflected off of the sea just barely brushing its edge. The shining facades of new elevator doors leaned against a wall near to the tools; the entrance to the elevators boarded on the outside and barred from within by a button now dead. Still, nothing stirred. For two days it had sat with the tensely expected return of life.

The sliding doors closed behind Kevin, with the cut off pocket of cold sea-wind clinging to his jacket like phantom tentacles. A half-hour break hadn't been much, it had barely given him time to smoke a cigarette and walk down to the corner store for a cup of coffee and a microwaved egg and cheese sandwich, but it was the best that he had had in the last eight hours, and would have to do.

The Long Shift

His ankles ached and he could feel the inflamed flesh bulging against the tight synthetic canvas, the grinding of eyelets with each step. Why had he decided to treat himself to new boots on that, of all weeks? Because one of the brawling drunks had bled all over his old pair. That was why. But bloody comfort was better than crisp pain. Maybe he could get Mary to stop by his place and bring the old pair.

Benches across from the doors to the shuttle lot sat vacant, between them a stack of Weekly's were piled in their box untouched, just as they had been the week before and the week before that. The entrance to the Mardi Buffet stood shuttered tight, the dull light filtering through the slits in steel like squinting eyes; inside, rows of steam-trays were gathering dust, the salt air tarnishing silver, the grime of forced air grew in corners, but still the lights stayed on to give the impression of a temporary, and very expected, closure. But nothing closed in this town unless it was

for the long haul, and it had been a very long haul for the buffet indeed.

"Hey Karl," he said as he approached the Members Services desk. "Maria, how's Lisa been?"

The casino tended to hire the multi-lingual for the desk. Maria was from the city but spoke Spanish, which came in handy in that neighborhood; Karl was from Austria, or maybe Germany, one of those former bad guys. Kevin could never remember which.

"She's thirteen, so an asshole."

"I doubt any of us were any better. Just look at Karl here, clearly a reformed total asshole."

"At least I can say reformed."

"There's something to be said for consistency. Alright guys," he said and turned toward the floor. "If there's anything you need, just let me know."

"Hey Kev?" Maria called.

"Yeah?"

"There's been some guys selling dope

next to the employee lot. You think there's anything you could do about it?"

"I'll check it out as soon as I clock back in."

A temporary partition, printed with the sights of New Orleans revelry, blocked the view of the gaming floor from the walkway. It stretched almost unbroken along the full two-block length of the casino; it made the walkway look that much dimmer, with its lighting already low to keep eyes on the tables and slots. Gaps, where the partition bent along a curve in the walkway, sent daggers of vibrancy across the glittering purple and gold carpet. In the last three months he had seen the full length of the partition replaced, piece by piece, at least twice; whether a spilled drink, an asshole kid's tag, or the splatter of some bodily fluid, something inevitably caused the re-placement of a section.

Kevin stopped at one of the breaks in the partition, The Big Easy bar, and stepped over the velvet rope blocking it off. He

reached over the little circular oasis in the floor, grabbed a Red Bull, and took a step down from the other side. Lights flashed in long rows from atop slot machines on the desolate gaming floor, and the voices of celebrity chefs droned on in rotation to come on down to restaurants that had, for the most part, yet to reopen.

In the months without footfall from anyone not employed by the casino, the carpet had gathered a coating of fine sand particulate, giving a frosted look without depth or dimension. Without the intrusion of people, the island was already reclaiming itself. A brush of motion flitted in the corner of his eye, and he jumped. At the end of the row, a scantily clad woman winked and pointed at him in an eternal loop from the big touchscreen, the current winning-pool shimmering at zero over her flowing hair. His heart beat in free-form erratics, and he rubbed dry eyes, and chugged the rest of his drink. *Keep moving, keep sharp.* Stools sat flipped onto the

The Long Shift

top of game tables between black, plastic ashtrays, and a vacuum sat in the middle of the walkway between slot rows. He dragged it along, though that was surely in violation of some union rule, and left it beside a maintenance hall next to the east-side windows.

A line of rolling chairs waited under the awning on the boardwalk, the operators calling to tourists from farther out on the boards or huddled together to smoke against the big plate-window away from the wind. Gulls called and pecked at each other on the far rail, confused by the lack of snatchable meals.

The only nonnative activity was the small groups shuffling along, light coats pulled high and tight against the sharp winter gusts tearing off of a sea so cold that even the color had fled. Red slips of paper poked from their pockets as they hurried toward tables with some action. Cigarettes poked out from most of the tight-lipped mouths, and the distrustful,

darting eyes would have given them away from a mile, even if the inadequate clothes hadn't. If you were local, the presence of a mark could be felt like a static shock.

"Come on down to the Flavor City Country Cookoff," blared the voice of a certain celebrity chef that Kevin found particularly unbearable, "for extreme tastes and the sound of your favorite hits! Whether you want Cajun Spice Steak Strings, or my favorite Taco Fried Rice, it'll be the bling-blang-bomb, for sure. *I need to rock down to Fla-vor City with you, compadre.*"

The Members Services desk was empty as he passed back along the west wing, a cup of coffee still steaming at Maria's station. He knew that there was a shot of Bailey's instead of cream in there, and was tempted to steal it away for himself. Anything to keep the doldrums of monotony away.

He stopped at the wall across from the Mardi Buffet and watched, waiting for

The Long Shift

a vagrant to pass out of view of the sliding doors, before he pressed on a section of wainscoting and felt the soft pop of the latch. He gripped inside the one-inch opening, pulled the door open, and slipped inside before the door sighed shut and the lock clicked.

He hated the back hall. When they were busy, yes it was a break from the throbbing masses of those anxious to gamble and those anxious to be far away from the memory that they had lost it all, but now, with the walkways desolate, it just showed how far below the nonexistent gamblers an employee's position was considered. Damp and cold, with nothing but grey primer to decorate steel floors and concrete ceiling and walls. As Brutalist as possible, the air wasn't even like the sweet smells pumped into the other side of the wall. Back in the hall, it was nothing but mildew, salt, and knowing at you were one wrong step away from the end.

Kevin's boots thudded on the stairs as

he made his slight hobble up to the second floor, avoiding the handrail that he had instinctively grabbed enough times to know that it was horribly sticky from human oils never cleaned. Overhead, one of the lights behind a tight security cage flickered, and the whole stairwell hummed with the electricity of the building between advertisements for restaurants and hot slots. Not even there, where no guest could ever stumble into, was he able to escape the constant barrage of consumerism. He came to the plain, grey door, with its plate that had once said 'SECURITY' painted over so many times that even the grooves of the letters were lost. He closed his eyes for a moment to steel his resolve, pressed down the handle, and entered.

"Come on down to the Flavor City Country Cookoff," the back hall speakers clamored as the door shut.

"Can't we turn that asshole off?" Kevin asked. "I mean, Flavor City wasn't even finished being built when we got bought last

year, and they've done fuck all to finish it since."

"How else will we know where to get Chocolate Marshmallow Calzone Bolts, or whatever nonsense he's hawking?" Bryan, a mass of flesh and uniform, with feet propped up on the control desk, said while still turned toward the screens.

Kevin laughed, and hung his jacket on the open hook, Bryan's reeking of old whiskey and sweat next to it.

"I swear to God, that's what was pumping through when you were on vacation. Fuckin' Chocolate Marshmallow Calzone Bolts. The fuck is a Calzone Bolt, anyway?" he continued.

Kevin checked the guest manifests, a long list of vacant gaps save for a few here and there on the sixth floor. Two-hundred rooms in the belly of this behemoth, this towering pinnacle at the edge of the sea, and only seven were taken. Normal practice was to spread the rooms whenever possible; a practice designed to give the

feeling of a staff dedicated to the guest's every pampered whim while distancing one from the possible newlywed fighters. The strange thing was that there, on the end of the west wing was a block of three rooms side by side.

"What's up with this block on six?" Kevin asked.

"Some hippies or Krishnas or something. All came in while you were on rounds carrying a bunch of boxes and shit," Bryan said, diligently cleaning his earbuds.

"But why would they choose a block at the west wing? There's plenty on the east with a view of the water."

"Do I look like a damned hippie? How in the hell would I know?"

A shuffling and murmur of voices came from behind the closed door to Kevin's office, and he turned toward Bryan with a questioning look as the handle clicked and door opened. Tom Belson came out with Mr. Huntzinger, the new head of Guest Services after the purchase, facing Kevin just

The Long Shift

long enough to give his classic 'don't you have something that you should be doing?' look. Tom loved when the higer-ups came by, because it gave him even more of an excuse to be the vile rat that he was born to be.

They stood in the corner, with Mr. Huntzinger laughing at something that Kevin hadn't caught. His mouth looked too long, too accentuated, like some slightly surreal portrait, especially when he laughed. Kevin expected to see a river of oil, or the rough skin of some elephant's trunk to emerge from the gaping orifice at any moment.

Tom pulled a pen from the cup at the log station and spun it between his fingers, talking about the membership to Seaview that he just secured, and the difficulty of the fifteenth hole. Either way, it was pretty obvious that they weren't going anywhere soon.

"Hey Tom, can I talk to you for a minute?" Kevin asked.

Zachary Von Houser

Tom swung his arm out toward the office in a theatrical motion of acquiescence and waited for Kevin to enter first.

"I'm kind of busy, so make it quick," Tom said, leaning against the desk.

Kevin felt his mettle waver, as Tom hadn't shut the door when they had entered, and spoke in just over a whisper.

"Well, you know, it's not anyone's--"

"I just said that I'm a busy man, Adams. Now out with it," Tom shouted. He was playing it up for his guest, like they had never had a casual conversation in their lives, and Kevin knew that he was doomed.

"I haven't had more than an hour off at a time for the last three days," he kept his voice low in a hope of steering Tom's in that direction, "and I was just hoping I could get a few hours off tonight to grab some real shut-eye."

He could see from the satisfied droop in Tom's eyelids that he was savoring this.

"Time off? Do you happened to remember what this weekend is?" he said,

The Long Shift

louder than before.

"Time off? Oh, no, no, no, no," the voice came hurrying from behind Kevin. "It's Chinese New Year, son. That's why we need you more than ever."

"I'm sure we must have misheard him, Mike," Tom said. "Explain to Mr. Huntzinger that we misheard, Kevin."

"I understand that it's New Year, but--"

"But nothing, my records show this is the busiest group of days in the slow season." Huntzinger placed a long, thin hand on Kevin's shoulder. "How many years have you been here for?"

"Eleven."

"Eleven years, then you should know as well as anyone that this is the bump we need to make it until Memorial Day." Heavy cologne wafted off of him and enveloped Kevin, the disregarding look on his face enough to break the bit of patience that Kevin's exhausted mind held.

"The gaming floor isn't open. How busy do you think Chinese New Year is go-

ing to be without gaming? They just going to line up for a grand old time at the vending machines?" He knew that he had said too much, to the wrong people, but it had just burst out.

"It doesn't matter what *you* think they're going to fucking do," Tom said, his voice a slab of cold slate. "What are you going to do, go to your rep? You're the one that asked, God damned begged, to be a supervisor when we got bought by Mr. Huntzinger's people. You're management now. Don't like it? Just *try* to find another casino to work at after you quit."

The pair walked out, Huntzinger's head shaking slowly, and just before they rounded the corner and were at the door to the stairs, Tom said, "sometimes you just need to show the whip, to remind 'em who's boss. So, the sixteenth hole..."

Bryan was pretending to be engrossed with the phone, as a slight mercy, when Kevin left his office. He grabbed his coat from the hook, checked the tuck of his

The Long Shift

shirt, and stopped for a second at the door to mutter, "I'm going on rounds."

He cut through the room service kitchen, where cooks worked knives smoothly at their stations or stirred huge pots boiling on burners; sixties soul played from a boombox coated with a thin layer of accumulated grease and pitted with steamed rust. Operators sat bored in a little room of glass walls, reading magazines or chatting in muted words.

The chef sat in her office, overworked and unaided, breaking down the price-points of a new menu that was unneeded but demanded by someone from above with no understanding of the industry. Strands of hair dangling from beneath her paper hat were pushed aside as she sliced away every penny she could. A move from community into isolated singularity, floating upward along the rungs until reaching a point where above and below worked at the constant grind of attempting to break

you. You were a cog to those above and corporate's stick to those below. Follow the word from higher ups too closely and you were a traitor--- and with what they asked, deservingly so; defend your people too well and corporate would find a weasel to turn your workers against you when it came time for yearly evaluation. Once you broke, and eventually they would assure that you did, the next in line would move up. Kevin knew the con only too well, the little 'supervisor' on his shirt above his name was a testament to that. He gave her a quick nod and worked east.

Passing a couple of busboys sharing a cigarette, he entered the east stairs. Although they were still cement and steel, signs that a situation could occur where this stairwell might be used by guests were clear. The walls were painted a seaside shade of mint, nonslip strips were adhered to the stairs, and at the landing to every floor a large window gave an immaculate view of the ocean. Even in a fire, the casino

The Long Shift

was only interested in the experience.

At the doorway to the fourth floor, he paused for a moment. Something, something so small as to be almost imperceptible, had caught his attention. He held his breath and put all of his focus on his ear at the door. On the other side, less than a whisper, he could make out a dry, scratching tap. He heard it, a dozen at a time, before a pause and the pattern would start once more. He let it run through twice before turning the knob and pushing the door inward. It moved no more than an inch before stopping dead against the clatter of metal on metal, something on the other side barely giving until unwilling to move any farther. The tapping noise had stopped as abruptly as the door had. He brought the walkie to his mouth, paused listening for a moment more and pressed the button.

"Hey Bryan, do you got eyes on four?"

"Yeah. What's up?"

"I heard something on the landing and

I can't get the door open, can you give a look?"

"Come on, I'm trying to watch a video of some ducks that are friends with a rabbit."

"I don't give a--"

"Fine, fine. Nope, nothing here."

"Are you sure? I know I heard something scratching on the other side and now the door's wedged shut..."

"Man, it's probably a mouse or a nudie mag flapping in the breeze, and I'm sure you *can't* get in. Those guys pile everything against the door when they leave so no one can get in and steal all their tools and shit. *Now*, if there's nothing else, they're showing the duck and rabbit their new house."

Kevin replaced the walkie and crouched down. On the floor sat a piece of heavy, tan canvas, a leather tag showing a notable tool company. He rubbed the cloth between his fingers and even such a light rustling pulled the fibers loose from each other; the strands tearing and crumbling

The Long Shift

under his touch, it fell to pieces and drifted to the floor.

As he ascended the stairs, the view at each landing took on greater grandeur. The dominance of land, and man's dominion, sank away into lesser significance. The sea grew as an unconquerable sheet of slate, with the rippling white ridges of waves only near to the shore as a wagging finger against hubris. As he reached the uppermost floor, Kevin had to crane his neck down to see even a small strip of sand, and he was in the Bienville Lounge.

Within the eminent glass cube, he stood in the center, lit a cigarette, and took it all in. All but forgotten for the last two years, anything requiring maintenance had long since been hauled away to some dark storage netherworld, and so there was nothing to intrude on his panorama, save for a lone table and ashtray in the center. From the west, the city was nothing but rooftops, a multicolor mosaic set in a grid just far enough away to lose its

bloated aspect, cars a glimmering stream of indefinite motion, all hemmed in by the reflective bay. The coastline, snaking along as a string of tan for miles into the horizon from two sides, towns growing less and less detailed, the intrusion of humanity less pronounced until it was a streak of discoloration. He took one last turn around and put out his cigarette.

Some corner boys were standing next to the entrance of the employee parking lot, just as Maria had said, but crossed the street as he approached. They would move back as soon as he was gone, eyeing employees as they came and left, making quick hand-offs to the twitchy addicts that shuffled in from the side streets, but what was he supposed to do? They lived in this part of town and, as far as they were concerned, he was simply a guest. No matter how many hours were spent on that block, how many miles he had walked in the same continuous circuit, he was, and

The Long Shift

always would be, an outsider.

Their world was a different, in some ways simpler, in some more complex, world. One that he could never understand no matter how long he was in it, just a more refined, more precise version of the idea that if you were born on the island you were a local. It wasn't something that you could move or marry into. It took but one look to pick out the phony.

He entered the parking lot and passed from the luxury cars of high management into the beat-up economy of the general workforce, before turning into a dead zone of the cameras, beside a withered juniper tree. "Fuck, that was dumb, Kevin," he said as he pulled the phone from his pocket. He pushed down the stress in his chest, lit a cigarette, and pressed the button.

"Hello?" Mary said, with that questioning inflection, even though he knew that his name had popped up as it rang.

"Hey, doll. So, I've got some bad news." He took a deep drag on his cigarette.

Zachary Von Houser

"I got all dressed up though, Kev."

"I know, Belson was just being a real prick. I couldn't even get a word in."

"It's fine. I'll call Angelo's and cancel the reservations."

The disappointment in her voice was dagger-sharp. Days without any real sleep. Days without seeing Mary for more than the couple of minutes when he had stopped by her work, and that was nothing more than following her from table to table as she dropped off drinks. Days of walking those damned floors, while Tom Belson stopped by whenever he felt, or when he knew someone high enough up would be there. They were days of blistering blood-pressure, of anonymity when recognition was deserved and recognition when anonymity was all that he wanted. Days pulled from his inventory of life, never to return.

"What about the fireworks?" he asked.

"What about 'em?"

"Why don't you meet me on the board-

walk out front for the fireworks? We can grab a quick bite after."

"Belson's going to let you take a break then?"

"Fuck Belson. Let's see him try and stop me."

The commissary was a quiet temple of steel and tile with a slight smell of lingering fruit. He leaned against the counter and waited. A knife lay on the prep table, its handle a protrusion of blistered, white plastic, beside a hotel pan piled high with forks and spoons. The bain-marie steam table was open with long sheets of plastic wrap protecting its innards from dust and bugs. A single dim lightbulb cast everything in a mourning pallor, the brushed steel barely giving off a shimmer. Abandonment was something that scarred places as well as people. Popping open the walk-in, a waft of old decay brushed past his face. The last sputtering hisses of the coffee machine sighed weakly, and Kevin poured

Zachary Von Houser

himself a large cup, slid the plastic sleeve back over the tall stack of Styrofoam, and took a tentative sip. It tasted of blackness and the quiet room, the can left behind when the kitchen was shut up more than a year before, but the seal had held a bit of pep inside the scoop.

A layer of dust clung to the penny slots, flickering the light of the neon rings mounted above. 'We still need to draw guests from the boardwalk.' The words that Huntzinger had said, on the first of many times that he had met Kevin and subsequently forgotten about, echoed through his head. Like they wouldn't be able to tell through the windows that it was all a show? "Only idiots assume that everyone else in the room is the dumb one."

He worked along the cage, receipts and transaction books, worthless and forgotten with the old logo, the old incorporation written below. A ring of keys hung above a row of tags with the printed photos of ca-

The Long Shift

shiers' faces. He saw them now and then at one locals bar or another these days, names half-remembered but the change in uniform to somewhere down the beach created an impassable gap.

As he tried the handle to the main cash box inside the cage, the roar of falling coins, pulled slot handles, and happy shouts rushed at him. He dropped his hand and hurried out onto the floor. Empty and motionless, only the flicker of graphics on screens met him. "I won!" A shout came through the cacophony, and Kevin looked up at the speakers. Out of that little box poured the madness of an addiction-and-adrenaline-filled floor.

"Fuck," he said, and rushed over to a phone in the maintenance corridor. He understood why the walkies only stayed on security channels, but at moments like this it would have been pretty convenient. Sitting his coffee down, he hurriedly dialed the extension and gave a questioning gesture to the cameras.

Zachary Von Houser

"What the hell is going on with the speakers in Zone Three?" he asked over the din, when someone finally picked up. "We've got a background track going loud. It sounds like the best day of the year down here."

"We've been getting power outages all day. They keep throwing up glitches all over, but we've got one of the electricians trying to figure it out. Lucky there's no one here to hear it, huh?"

"We'll look pretty dumb if someone comes in to the sound of winning and no winners. Won't we? So, maybe get on that shit, *huh*?"

"Done and... done." The sound effects of recording studio gamblers' joy and well-timed coins dropping suddenly cut out and were replaced once more by the unnoticeable music that was cheap enough for the casino's budget. "You know, you'll catch more flies with honey."

"And you know, you'll catch less shit if you do your damned job." The phone

The Long Shift

slammed into the cradle with the satisfaction that only an old corded phone can have, and for a moment his exhausted mind swam from the exertion.

He noticed the speckles of discoloration on the lid as his hand touched the cup, off-color dots haphazardly clinging to the lip. "The hell?" He asked, pried the lid off, and pulled back in revulsion as the contents came into view. Blooms of sickly green and dull grey mold lined the inside of the cup with islands of it floating atop the black coffee, where it had splashed them clear of the sides. Spores hovered in decrepit fog just above the surface, swirling in a solemn dance of corruption.

What could be trusted in this place? A skeleton crew trying to keep together the boards of a sinking ship. There were too many nooks, too many places for the cracks to start. It was a Sisyphean feat, and none could expect any different results.

Passing the elevator banks, a couple caught his eye. They both wore necklac-

es of bright red beads, their hair long and greasy looking. A price tag hung from the sleeve of the burgundy sweatshirt around the woman's waist. The man's eyes, pale orbs of mint with pinpoint pupils, the woman's were a deep brown near to black. They stared unblinking at him, the man's fingers slowly drumming against some piece of electronic equipment in his hands, a plastic bag bulging with round shapes in the woman's.

After so many years of turning on and off the precise-observer part of his brain, the switch had snapped away somewhere along the trip. So ingrained was it in his mind, that even a casual walk to the corner to get a pack of cigarettes pulled in a hundred details that would never be of use. Mary did her best to let it go in the beginning, his quick scan of someone at the bar from the corner of his eye, checking a shirt just above the waistband for a concealed weapon, or the crease in his brow as he worked something out, but the fact that

it drove her insane was now plainly clear. Still, better to have the odd quirks and idiosyncrasies out there than unhoned skills in here.

There was something about their indifferent calmness, like they knew something that he didn't, that pricked some part of Kevin's mind. The man's lips turned down within an unkempt beard as Kevin's hand instinctively went for the reassuring feel of his pepper spray.

"Fucking weirdos."

He walked around the back of an old-looking prop popcorn booth and slid through the thin hidden door. The corridor stunk of its contents, piles of trash bags sat in big plastic carts, stained brooms leaned against the wall next to mildewed mops. Kevin popped open the door at the far side, wedged a piece of wood into the bottom of its heavy steel mass, and stepped out onto the cold concrete.

The main dumpster was a hulking mass of metal, with green and white paint

bubbling and peeling on its sweating form. Noxious vapors hovered at its yawning opening and swayed ghastly in the breeze. Kevin sat on the upturned wooden box next to the coffee can overflowing with filters and cigar ends, and breathed in the decay of the only official outdoor smoking area. The eyes of two cameras kept a keen watch on him, unblinking toward any infraction. Bryan couldn't care less if he pulled out his phone, but Belson could always be a vulture over the shoulder. The way that the day was going, he would have to remember to lock up his phone when he got back, just in case Tom had a "random" check planned.

He tapped a cigarette loose from the soft-pack and pulled it free with his teeth. Even the stench, and the cold, and the discomfort of his seat couldn't keep his eyes from closing for a brief reprieve as the cigarette lit.

His mind wandered in the darkness behind his eyes. Images floated forward from

The Long Shift

the forest of synapses, sounds swirled in a comforting whisper. His bedroom, but with the wrong colored walls, was trembling with a blue glow coming in through the windows. Mary was there, asking what had happened to the sink. He rose from the bed, about to drop himself into that world, to accept the questions and the inconsistencies, when a searing pain alit from between his fingers and his eyes shot open.

"Fuck!" he shouted and threw the smoldering end of his cigarette against the stinking dumpster.

Kevin scanned but still wiped out the inside of the cup before pouring his coffee. Log work, the great bureaucratic processing of day in and out, was the one true shadow of his day. He didn't get into security to fill out form work, especially when there was so little to report. Leave that to some nerd in a cubicle. He had signed up for the action.

After dropping his phone in the lock-

box, he wrote up the speaker glitch, and a stirring of motion on one of the monitors caught his eye. It had been a long time since he had gotten any proper rest, and while he might be a bit twitchy he had never been one to see things that weren't there. He rubbed his eyes, feeling the thick fluid behind puffy lids, and panned the camera around. The hall sat still and quickly descended into darkness as he scanned away from the window.

"Fuckin' shit," he muttered and pulled his hand away from the control. "You know if they have anyone working on four right now?" he turned to Bryan and asked.

"Hell no, they aren't. I got into the wrong union. Time-and-a-half on weekends, no holidays, not even this one. Like they got any Chinese working their crews. Shit, I'd be having it easy."

Suddenly, as he was considering how to tell Bryan that he didn't do much anyway, another figure came into frame. A hood was pulled low over their head, and

The Long Shift

they clutched some darkened object as the hurried across the screen. Kevin grabbed the control, jerked it hard to the right, but by the time it responded the hall was once again clear.

"Well, I saw someone moving around up there. Want to go check it out?"

"*I* didn't see shit. You want to know so bad, be my guest."

Realizing that it could afford him enough time to pop out onto the boardwalk for the fireworks, Kevin pulled on his jacket, tested the walkie, and said, "Keep an eye on the monitor, huh?"

"What, you can't handle a couple of asshole kids tagging the walls and smoking a joint?" Bryan said, scrolling through pictures of friends on his phone, one of his earbuds in his ear.

"Just stay off your phone until I get back."

"Write me up Mister Management. I'm sure our steward misses you."

"Prick."

Zachary Von Houser

Kevin climbed the two flights of back hall stairs with a cold breeze drifting down around him. The door squeaked open and gave way to darkness. Kevin clicked on his flashlight and entered the little room. The ice machine sat, a quiet coffin of polished metal; the vending machine shrouding its treats in inky black. The door slid shut behind him and the lock clicked loudly, a rectangle of dark burgundy with only a keyhole to show its purpose.

He stepped out softly into the hall. Floor four, the renovation floor, the floors above and below were vacant as buffers for the sound. The elevators wouldn't stop anywhere between two and six, to avoid anyone accidentally getting off on the wrong floor and seeing anything to break the spell of indulgence. Overhead, where fixtures would have once illuminated the hall, wires hung from gaping wounds in the ceiling like long-dead vines. A dagger of light shone through the cracked door

The Long Shift

to the western guest stairs, blotting out quickly as Kevin pulled away the cord that held it propped. Plugged into an outlet beside his foot, the green light of a charging battery pack flickered its readiness. The air was thick with particulate, hovering in the beam of his flashlight and giving the hall the feel of stepping into television static.

The first door opened to a room of grim twilight. Beds, a tall-back chair, dresser, and even the faint raise of the room service menu lay under white, cloth tarps splattered with dry paint. Everything was ready to go for the instant that paint was dry and guests would retake the floor. Kevin passed across and wiped clear the dust from the window. Through the streak of visibility, the bay, a splatter of soot within the ochre fields of whithered reeds, stretched its fingers out in blackened veins of canals. As he looked out at the dying sun's spot of illumination in the overcast, that repetitious, scratching tap from earlier caught his ear. He searched under furniture and within

closets in the terminal light, coming no closer to the source.

When he returned to the hall, he was met with a smell of citrus, and cellars, and the deathly rot of sugars. Room after room was in the same state of preservation, with the same scratching tap, and the trailing smell of something formerly crisp but now churning within itself with decrepitude. He had been hardened by years of security work, but there was still a feel to vacant floors that left him uneasy. The feeling that only the living, with their noise and motion and distraction, could block out the past; that the moments compounded within confines, with just a bit less energy than the action of the present, and, with that action lacking, the past could grab some hold. That it could dig hooks into those gaps that are usually filled by the presence of other lives.

Approaching the bend in the hall into the east wing, the smell grew stronger. His eyes stung and lungs tingled. Heavy

The Long Shift

it hung around him, oranges and corruption, each room seeming to exhale a little more, and within each room the sound grew louder. Some instinct, far beyond and far before anything that he had learned in his life brushed the hairs on his arms. After leaving the last room before the bend, the sound also seemed to follow into the hall, mixed with some parched shivering chatter, it leaked into the back of his skull. A trickle of sweat running through his hair, he took a calming breath and turned.

Only the void met his gaze, his flashlight beam dying quickly in the dusty air, but there *was* something. A something that could be nothing, but something to notice still. Along the wall between rooms, four slashes of burgundy ran crisp where they were wiped clean of dust.

He glanced down at his uniform to see if he had rubbed against the walls, but like everything on the floor, it had been sullied with a thin coat of its own dust. Mud caked in the creases of his clammy hands.

He could feel the muck thickening on his brow.

As quickly as these details were taken in, something was removed. Gone were the sounds, cleared was the air of that fetid smell.

The far end of the east wing was lit by a sickly diffused light oozing in through the window. Beyond, the sea was an expansive sheet of crinkled tin glittering in the last reflective rays of a tired day. The bobbing lights of boats flashed red and green as they ventured off or returned home. Black specks circled languidly in the distance, their cawing cries long lost before reaching his ears.

With the comfort of his nearing proximity to that little light, as he touched the knob to a room, came the sound of a soft hum from farther down the hall. He walked carefully, and as he grew closer, the sound became more distinct and recognizable; the mechanical noise, embracing in its fa-

The Long Shift

miliarity, of a generator.

He cracked his neck and stretched his shoulders back, having not even noticed how hunched they had become. He resumed his practiced posture of authority. At room four-eighteen the noise grew even more crisp, at four-sixteen he could hear the murmur of voices, and at four-fourteen he stopped. Multiple voices were distinguishable from each other, a few deep and at least one higher.

Kevin stepped up to the door, checked his pepper spray, and pulled out his master key-card. Even if some of the power had been cut to that wing, the batteries on the locks should still be functional. Thank God for fire codes.

He put his ear to the door and picked out at least three voices. Three on one weren't the best odds, but a strong tone and a handful of pepper spray could go a long way in his industry. Besides, a uniform, even one coated in dust, tended to make people second guess throwing a

punch for fear of there being some greater charge than simple assault.

No matter the odds, he would rather catch them in the act. If you caught them, they were more likely to follow along. Given the chance to flush the drugs, they would always act like you were a cop and didn't have anything on them. Then, when you showed that you didn't have to *exactly* follow the guidelines of the police, things could quickly get messy. Fight or flight, you never knew what they would pick. It was easier to give a disapproving look, take their stash and kick them out. No paperwork needed, no reason for a brawl, or, even worse, potential daddies with lawyer friends. Things could get very messy indeed.

The smell of the generator wafted from under the door, and while the reason that they would be running it was still an unknown variable, it would mask the sound of the lock disengaging and give him that little bit more of an edge. With the can of

The Long Shift

spray in one hand, he pushed the card into the slot. His elbow twitched. The hum of the generator rumbled through the knob. The light above the card flashed green. He twisted the cold, metal knob and pushed.

A group of teenagers piled onto the couch by the window getting stoned; a cheap john and his less than particular date, not even concerned enough to pull the tarp from the bed; some squalid cluster of junkies breaking up a score in privacy. Those were all things that he expected. He never expected the dazzling array of lights filling the room, the slovenly group of four, nor the greasy smoke of burning incense and generator exhaust.

Lamps filled the room, plugged into a series of black, metal boxes with small knobs and digital readouts, dimming and illuminating in an off-timed rhythm. Overhead, the lights had been cleared of their covers, which had been tossed into a disorderly pile of broken glass in the corner

of the room. In the adjoining bedroom, a pile of televisions blared the madness of static. Covering each wall, lines of string were tacked into precisely distanced rows, hanging rectangles of vibrant red in meticulous spacing. In the center of the room, the small dining table sat, with a chair at either side; all of the other furniture had been piled into the far corners of the room. The group didn't appear to be frightened, or even startled, instead, they stood there, one on his left, one on the right, the man and woman from the elevators ahead at the table, all with that regimented aloofness that Kevin had seen before.

"What in the hell is all of this?" he asked and reached for one of the strings of dangling red paper. "You can't--"

"Sir, I wouldn't," the man at the table said.

Who did he think he was to be giving commands? Kevin was sick of being on this floor, sick of the way that it had played tricks on his mind, sick of the whole

The Long Shift

damned shift, and he turned to tell him who was in charge, just in time to see the last moment of the lamp's arc into the left side of his head.

As he woke, around him was a dazzling radiance that made him flinch. He pushed his head to the side, his adjusting eyes half-blind, and heard someone shout something from behind. His senses were taking things in, but the processing wasn't working in time. He would hear or see something, and a second or two later would grasp some aspect of it. Nothing was complete. It was as though he were translating his hearing, his vision, from some half-understood language.

"...nothing got in? How ca..." the words trickled.

Slowly, thoughts of where he was came back to him. He felt a chair at his back, his knees were bent, feet touching the floor. An iron heat radiated from his temple. He lolled his head to a point where it was

vaguely facing forward. The slightest motion threw the thoughts from his mind and turned the inside of his skull to an inescapable seething slosh. With the greatest effort, he calmed the motion and opened his eyes. He was seated at the table. Dark blurs of motion slowly grew crisp in his vision. The lights seemed less insufferable, the structure of the room developed, he tracked the silhouettes as they slowly grew in definition.

"...ink could possibly stop it? Are you a nonbe..."

Kevin tightened the muscles of his hands, trying to bring the tips of his fingers to thumbs. They were close, the synapse time making the crude formation of fists instead. What day did he do laundry? No. Focus. He was at work, he was sitting, his head hurt. His eyes closed. Sleep. Just a few minutes would clear his mind. No. No sleep. His head hurt, either the pain or the reforming memory turned his stomach. Oranges, he didn't know if he smelled

them now or remembered.

"We ask you to speak to us, through your humble vessel, from the darkness. We beg you to show us that which none can speak of after knowing."

Walking the corridor. At the door. The brilliance of light.

"We implore, you who know all, to grant us even a glimpse of true knowledge."

The stink of the room. Memories locked together faster and faster.

"What is your name, great knower?"

Kevin cracked his eyes, letting them adjust slowly. Faces came into focus, ropey hair, eyes wild with anticipation. He slowly worked his hand from his lap. Two of them moved out of either side of his vision. Only the man at the table, now shirtless, and the woman were in view. He slid his hand to his hip, feeling for the can of pepper spray. An empty pouch hung there.

"I'm glad that you're back with us Mister..." He glanced down at Kevin's name tag. "Adams. Hmm. A bit anticlimactic of a

name for one of the first to see such greatness, isn't it? Anyway, you'll not be finding that little can there, Mister Adams. My associate at your side has it primed and ready in case you decide to become... less than hospitable to our pursuits."

Kevin twisted his head to see a skinny man, draped in a red robe, with his thumb on the pepper spray canister aimed at Kevin's face. He overshot turning his head back and caught the edge of another man, of similar dress and build, a long blade extending from his hand.

"Yes, Mister Adams, we have you guarded quite well. Now, we had no interest in hurting you... or anyone, for that matter, but we couldn't have you breaking the barrier. It is, after all, for your protection as well as ours. Your walkie talkie, that has also been removed from you, for your protection as well."

"This is not going to go well for you," Kevin slurred.

"How wrong you are. It will now go

The Long Shift

quite well, but if you were allowed to follow through your misguided instincts it
would have gone quite poorly for us all."

"You assholes--"

"No need for profanity Mister Adams.
I can assure you that I have no ulterior to
what I say. You see, if I had allowed you to
tear down even a portion of the barrier, we
would have all been in a grave state." He
rubbed his fingers into a tin on the table
and brought them to his chest. "It is the red
that keeps us safe. It keeps *out* those that
are *out* and *in* those that are *in*." His hands
worked deftly across his chest, the fingertips twisting mad swirls and quick daggers
of black onto his skin. Kevin noticed that
the eyes weren't really green, but more of
a dusty blue, spiked with hazel near to the
pupil. At either side of him, a pile of oranges sat on the table.

"It keeps out who?"

"Those from beyond. They are repelled
by the red, on this day of all days especially.
This is the day of their greatest strength,

and also their greatest weakness toward that which is abject to them. It has been spoken of by the great teachers since the beginning."

"Since the beginning," those other three said in unison.

"It is one of their greatest repellents. So, those that are allowed within are trapped, like iron bars, and those outside are kept from."

Kevin turned his eyes toward the array of lights behind the man, their oscillation swaying in pitch.

"There is a feel to illumination, Mister Adams. A feel and a charge like that of life. All electricity has it, but the dispersing of the photon, like the breath of exuberance, it draws them. They are vaguely drawn toward the whole of this building, especially those that perish here. The life, the motion, the subtle minutia of life, they breathe it in like air. They become addicted to the essence of life, as though it could keep them a part of it, and just like any addict, they

The Long Shift

grow to only know their hunting grounds to feed such an addiction. So, when a place that was at one point a constant well of sustenance for them, such as this, is suddenly vacant, they become ravenous with hunger. It is an unfortunate aspect that those spirits drawn toward the force of life, just like the living addict, will do anything for a taste when the climate is lacking. They are drawn to any energy that they can find, Mister Adams, and will do anything to get it."

The overhead lights flickered a stuttered break.

"Luckily, your men left this generator for us. Your power here is *quite* unpredictable."

Kevin shifted slightly to his side and the man with the pepper spray tensed visibly. There would be no quick action to save him.

"The rheostat boxes, well, the fluctuation seems more real to them. Nothing in life is a constant level. We are always in

a great state of oscillation from the point of birth." The man brought his hands in to a pose of benediction. "Now, as we move into our final phase of contact, there is a warning that I must give you Mister Adams. It is not an *alpha* warning, there is no threat to your machismo, but a warning of the most due diligence, in that I wish no harm to come of you. No matter what you see, no matter what you feel, do not open the door."

Kevin slowly looked behind him and saw the red tags covering the door.

"The barrier must stay unbroken until the birth of the morning light. It is the order of the ancients."

"Order of the ancients," they mimicked.

The man dropped into a hushed incantation that Kevin couldn't perceive. Slowly, solemnly, the volume crept upward, with letters and syllables indiscernible. The woman ran some smoldering bundle of noxious hate over him with head bowed. The tips of the fingers across from Kevin

The Long Shift

grew to a periwinkle shade in a tremulous tapping on the table. The man's hand rose and smeared the symbol on the left side of his chest and head lifted. Capillaries spread oil-dark in eyes searching the ceiling.

"We beseech you to speak through this willing vessel," the woman said.

Lights flickered. Again the man's hand rose to his chest, and pink lines leapt up in the wake of nails digging downward across the flesh. A low rumble vibrated through Kevin's seat. Small splotches formed across the pale skin of the man's face; his eyes shivered in their sockets and the blue went the color of old swamp water in a jar. The hand moved more quickly across the flesh, pink lines going red through the smeared symbols, the other hovering over one of the piles of oranges. An obscuring haze grew inward from the corners of the far window. The man's teeth chattered in front of the rolling tongue. The generator groaned and fought, and a haze of black smoke slithered from its frame.

The lights grew in intensity. Thin red smears trailed the hand, working in measured time. Smoke began to snake its way around the light bulbs.

"Please great knower--" She started.

Then came the drumming. Through the walls he could hear it, that dry, scratching tap he had heard before. But now, not the work of one, but dozens, all working in rhythm with the blood-smeared hand across from him. Some small motion grew in the pile of oranges below the hovering hand.

"P-please..." Her grip trembled, and ash snowed down upon the man. Her eyes watered with lids pulled back tight.

Flesh grew pulpy below the raking nails. Cracking light bulbs hissed. The oranges shifted as blooms of mold sprouted upon them. A grinding groan drew up from the generator. Kevin looked from face to face at either side of him, but they were lost to a look of awe and astonishment. A snapping crack drew Kevin's attention

The Long Shift

forward, to teeth chipping and splitting in the chattering mouth. Blood ran down in rivulets as the flesh of the man's chest was gouged away in strips by the crimson-smeared hand.

Shards of tooth sputtered from the mouth and blood rolled from the corners of cracked, white lips, as chunks of tongue, trapped between the quick chomp of jagged teeth, were bitten away. The hand above the shriveled pile of citrus mold had grown black, the skin on the forearm patched with desiccated green and bulbs of white and gray fuzz. The lips were drawn back and withered, spots of flesh on the cheeks dissolving away. The stench of rotting fruit made him gag. The woman's eyes were unseeing, cataracts fogging and black mold spreading across the desiccating whites, as spores floated up from the man's dying flesh. A mist of blood sprayed from the convulsing mouth, and the flesh had been peeled to muscle by digging nails across his chest.

Zachary Von Houser

The stuttering thud of seizing steel came from the generator, the lights flickered, and a clatter of metal came from behind. Kevin turned and saw the knife laying on the floor. Both men had fled to the corners of the room, their backs pressed tight. One had fists held tight against his eyes, the other was searching mechanically for some savior to appear.

Kevin knocked the chair over as he stumbled back, the spell of astonishment broken, and ran over to the man that had held the pepper spray.

"We've got to go," he said, waving his hand before the vision that still searched through it. "Come on!"

A scream pierced the room, and Kevin's head shot to see the woman clawing at her eyes, the skin all around them clustered with mold. The man was still in his seat, digging deep into the musculature of his chest, the other hand mummified uselessness over a pile of indiscernible grey-green mold, his head back with blood

The Long Shift

spurting out with each breath.

He grabbed his walkie from a pile of broken glass as he gripped the doorknob. The strings tacked across the frame snapped and the red paper tags fluttered down around his face like cherry blossoms.

The dry tapping came from the darkness of the long hall as he backed away. His hand went to the flashlight loop and felt its empty void. The ambient light cascaded from the boardwalk, and however sallow and meager, it drew him closer. His eyes searched the great shadow, an equal fight of hoping and not hoping to see what was making that noise. A noise that drew audibly closer as Kevin hoped to at least keep the pace.

He heard the pop of doors opening in the void. Some fog of particulate floating into the dull light. His stomach churned.

Doorknobs rattled at his side, that putrid fruit smell wafting in like a slow wave. The only thing that he knew, the only part

of his brain not deadened by shock, was that which told him to keep backing away. The distant call of screaming gulls the murmur of far off voices shouting in revelry, the clamor of winning bells and calls from the Ferris wheel. His back hit the window with a dull thud. Silhouettes shifted and grew closer, motion darker than the dark. The dark fear of the nightmare void, that spot of malignancy in the mind since birth, that pit of rot that terrorizes before the first thoughts of humanity, splintered through his mind in the confirmation of truth. The sound, he could feel it when his teeth touched, the dryness seeping into his brain, its volume grew. The only thing louder was the beating of his heart. The weight in his hand barely hinted to him at its existence. He looked down at the black rectangle with fleeting cognizance and brought it trembling to his mouth.

"Bryan... Fuck... Bryan do you read?"

Doorknobs thudded desperately.

"Bryan, bud, I need you to answer."

The Long Shift

A vice clamped on his throat.

The vague hints of limbs swayed and shifted, passing through space with a weightless ease.

"Damnit Bryan! Do you read?"

He could see it, knew how things were happening floors below. The monitors ignored, earbuds firmly in place, Bryan's eyes locked to the phone, the walkie laying on the board, words crackling through the speaker unheard.

And then the chorus of screams started from within the room.

The walkie dropped from his hand. He could hear the anguish, hear the crescendo of horror, as it rose to its peak. The cries bounced along the abysmal hall. The smashing clatter of lamps overturning, the culmination of deception, cut through the walls. He wished that it would stop. Thought that he would do anything for them to quiet. Until the moment that it did. The screams dulled to filial cries, to almost imperceptible groans that would have

been lost to the scratching taps and chatters if not for pitch. Then, he was left with only the sound of a world beyond.

Like a slow saw blade cutting in the winter, the sound engulfed his body. They moved closer, impossibly thin limbs occasionally passing close enough to gain definition. He felt deathly dullness at the end of his nerves. The thudding wind pressed the window into his back, driving him closer to the things approaching in the murk.

Rattling metal drew his attention. At his side, behind the leaning sheets of drywall and scaffolding, behind the piles of tool bags and buckets of screws of in front of them, shaking in the turning tunnel of wind, was the stairwell door. He threw a bucket of screws onto its side, the twists of shining metal glimmering across the dusty carpet, and rolled it away. Door handles around him clicked down, one after the other, the hinges barely whispering as the first inches of opening spread. Boxes were scattered, pieces of sheet-metal tossed

The Long Shift

aside, their jagged edges slicing into his palms. Clamoring applause rained through the window. He grabbed the handles of a heavy tool bag and pulled, its canvas heft catching on the carpet. The doors struggled open a fraction more. As he dragged at the worn nylon handles, the barest hint of deathly visage grazed the weak light.

He focused on the work, set his mind to it so that it wouldn't simply break. From the corner of his eye he saw them, skeletal limbs jutting from the moldering remnants of jackets and pants, moving slowly toward him. Ivory fingertips slid around the edge of open doors. His muscles screamed with the effort, joints popped as they wrenched apart. The last bag pulled clear, he could sense their proximity, he felt the rough fibers of the bag slip against his sweaty flesh, and he tumbled to the floor.

A fog of dust sifted around him. The tips of decaying toes hovered just above the carpet. Rotting jackets sat upon too-thin limbs, the decrepit fibers crumbling

and bare, mold-eaten oranges bulging from holes in deteriorating pockets. They waited in a curving wall of end-stage decay a bare few feet away; a noxious, shifting mass filling the width of the hall. He pulled himself up, wanting to go out on his feet at their final push forward.

They levitated there, running desiccated fingers down their ribs, the exposed bones at the fingertips drumming that dry, rasping tap. A gray and green fuzz of mold covered the whole of their dried remains, with their cavernous, skin-peeled chests. Teeth chattered as jagged points in lipless mouths. The ceaseless energy, the animalistic tension, even in the gaps of their eyeless sockets he could feel it burn. He could feel the vibrating drive for his flesh, his energy, his life-force, but for some reason the daren't move forward. What miracle had held back their wrath?

Across the seething shoulders under dusty black cloth, between the skull-like heads with their patches of thin, stringy

The Long Shift

hair, he saw himself and the answer. The new door for the elevator leaned against the wall, a great perfect mirror, yet to be scuffed or scratched. He stood in this reflection, an image of humanity in a bog of death, the sea and sky a block of darkness behind him, his body bathed in the red light of the exit sign. He looked down at his hand, dumb with luck, and basked in the crimson hue.

Barely three feet away the drywall and scaffolding leaned against the door. He could see the light from the gap beneath it. He could almost smell the fresh air. They shifted in only the most minute way, as he took a step toward it. The heat of rot was in his nostrils and a viscousness was filmed over his eyes. The weak spot of the whole pile, the unending sound of each of those creatures, he picked up everything simultaneously. The great grandness of existence, the singular notion of life, it was all focused onto this one point, this one place, and no other. He slid his hand outward.

Inches, agonizing inches, they grew between his body and hand. His mouth was coated in dead paste. His eyes refused to keep their focus. *Just a bit farther*. The door pressed like a breath, each heave of wind nearly bringing the edge of the dry-wall sheet to his fingers. The edge brushed his skin, the red light dissolved from the tips of his fingers, and it was the moment of truth. He lunged toward it, fingertips desperate for purchase on the back of the sheet, just an instant's action. But in that instant, his arm emerged from the red to the shoulder, a clawed hand slashed at him, and a fire welled in his flesh.

Pulling a protective hand away from his arm, four lines appeared on the black sleeve. They grew paler, with dots of gray growing outward from the stripes, the fibers snapping and falling away before his eyes. As the strips of fabric dropped away, he could see the skin below. Streaks of red went purple, then near-black, with darkened veins spreading forth. Bubbles

The Long Shift

formed on the flesh, growing upon each other, devouring and extending. He could feel the dark rot marching through him.

A heavy, wet thud pulled his attention from the arm; the weight of damnation behind it. The creatures grew even more animated. Plumes of mold fled the action of their grave-borne hands, the quick clawing mimicking the grinding of rocks. *Thud.* Their necks craned toward Kevin, the dried sinews bulging under the paper skin of their throats, and ruinous lips grazed the crimson glow. The bodies shivered and rocked against each other. *Thud.* The slightest flicker came from overhead. *Thud.* Starving teeth clashed, their action hastening in proximity to living flesh, desperate to tear and rend.

"What, you on break or something?" the voice cut through from the walkie laying eternally distant between the rows of rotten feet. "Belson's going to have your ass if you're not here when I get done."

The smell of the sea and decay, heavy

Zachary Von Houser

and wet in its fullness, pushed its way down the hall, and still the dull, squishing stomp drew closer. Grave-consigned hands swiped into the red glow at him, the digits curling afterward in pain. A soaked, pneumoniac breath rumbled from deep in the darkness. As Kevin thought of the absurdity of fate the red light stuttered its brilliance around him, and he felt the wind swept by a tearing for his throat. The window crashed against the back of his skull and the cold night seeped through his shirt. The calliope tinkled through the window, his breath heavy and burning in time with its sharp notes. He knew that somewhere out there, amongst the joy, amongst the mass of engulfed humanity, stood Mary. Close enough to see but impossibly far.

The light sputtered a strobe across him. A roar echoed down the hall. The acid in Kevin's stomach bubbled into his throat, and from the darkness appeared a pair of cracked and gnarled tusks, rotting strands of putrid seaweed dangling from their jag-

The Long Shift

ged lengths. Perdition had come, and knew his face. His head swam, hand gripped the edge of the window, and the light gave one choking stammer into death. Leaden stomps rushed toward him in blindness, he felt bony hands gripping at his arms, digging at his stomach.

He could see nothing, but felt, knew their all-encompassing grasp at him, their impurity burning its way into his very be-ing, those hulking footfalls quaking the floor, and a screeching whistle wracked the hall. It came as a dull haze, showing only the faintest outlines of his ruin. The claws continued their crazed pace, his flesh sizzling.

Then came the bang. The fireworks erupted. Skeletal hands dug at empty eye sockets. The dead fell back, ripping at each other to escape the detonations. As the tide of death parted he saw it there, a mad-ness that leaves no whole mind in its path. Each explosion was a snapshot of condem-nation. A massive jaw with pitted fangs of

rot extended in agony. Eyes that had been born in the abyss of darkness smoldered as decadent fur fell in clumps. The tusks clashed from side to side as a great paw rose in hope of blocking the light. Red and gold and blue, the hall was bathed in color as that horror pulled away with joints popping and breaking in sagging skin.

He sat there, his chest heaving in the rot-spotted fabric of his shirt, when the light flickered on. The celebration had come to an end and a hushed mutter wafted from the boardwalk. The calliope tinkled its repetitious song. The bell of the high striker rang in the distance. The little green light of his walkie glowed against the carpet. Dust hovered softly in the calm light, he lifted and stared at the flesh of an arm unmarked by gouges or pestilence, and the elevator door reflected a sky of stars over the sea.

THE END

THE END

THE END

THE END